THE ASSETS

About the author

Ted Allbeury was a lieutenant-colonel in the Intelligence Corps during World War II, and later a successful executive in the fields of marketing, advertising and radio. He has been writing since the early 1970s: he is best known for his espionage novels, but has also published one highly-praised general novel, *The Choice*, and a short story collection, *Other Kinds of Treason*. His novels have been published in twenty-three languages, including Russian.

Ted Allbeury's most recent novel is *The Reckoning*.

The Assets

Ted Allbeury

CORONET BOOKS
Hodder & Stoughton

First published in Great Britain in 2000
by Hodder and Stoughton
A division of Hodder Headline
First published in paperback in 2001
by Hodder and Stoughton

A Coronet Paperback

10 9 8 7 6 5 4 3 2 1

A CIP catalogue record for this title
is available from the British Library.

ISBN 0 340 77055 4

Printed and bound in Great Britain by
Mackays of Chatham PLC, Chatham, Kent

Hodder and Stoughton
A division of Hodder Headline
338 Euston Road
London NW1 3BH

To my brave and beautiful wife, Grazyna Maria,
who died a few weeks after I finished this book.

Like truthless dreams, so are my joys expir'd
And past return are all my dandled days;
My love misled, and fancy quite retir'd
Of all which pass'd the sorrow only stays.

My lost delights, now clean from sight of land,
Have left me all alone in unknown ways;
My mind to woe, my life in fortune's hand
Of all which pass'd the sorrow only stays

As in a country strange, without companion,
I only wail the wrong of death's delays,
Whose sweet spring spent, whose summer well-nigh done
Of all which pass'd only the sorrow stays.

Whom care forewarns, ere age and winter cold,
To haste me hence to find my fortune's fold.

Sir Walter Raleigh

I would remind you that extremism
in the defence of liberty is no vice!

Barry Goldwater

Speech accepting the presidential nomination 17 July 1964

Chapter One

When the wooden structure had been made at the small workshop in San Antonio, Texas, it had been intended for use as a garden shed. But its fate was to end up as the interrogation room for US Army Intelligence at Inchon in North Korea. Inchon was the collecting point for US prisoners of war who had been released as part of the deal between Washington and the Democratic People's Republic of North Korea. Most of the ex-prisoners were processed quickly and sent on to Pusan and home. But a few ended up in the wooden shed for more detailed interrogation.

There was a simple wooden table and several canvas chairs of the kind that film directors are supposed to favour. And there were three men. A US Army Intelligence lieutenant named Rosen, in clean and pressed tropical uniform despite the snow outside. A haggard-looking man sat opposite him, his mind obviously far away, the remnants of his uniform tattered and foul-smelling. The third man was in a chair in the far corner, listening and watching. Watching for any kind of response from the ex-prisoner with the far-away look.

Lieut. Rosen spoke slowly and carefully, with what in army terms would be considered a friendly tone of voice.

He had asked all the standard questions without a reply to any of them. But he was trained to be patient when interrogating. Especially when the subject was one of your own men.

He went through the litany of name, rank, unit. What happened to your dog tags? Is there anyone you'd like to contact? In the army or at home? And where was home?

He would have been disappointed to know that his subject didn't even hear what he was saying and was not aware of where he was.

Released prisoner RP7094 was still back in the dark in the cage. Listening to the screams in the other cells. Trying to make out whether the angry curses were in Chinese or Korean. All his fingers had been broken during the dozens of interrogations, his jaw had been fractured and there were burns on his skeletal rib-cage. He prayed sometimes that it would be the Chinese not the Koreans who interrogated him next. Talking softly but not persuasively of the privileges he would have from simple cooperation. And the same litany of questions. Name, unit, rank but no question about his dog tags. They already had them and he still had the long, curving wound on his neck from where they'd ripped off the string that had held the tags.

Finally he had been led away gently by the third man to a small cubicle with a camp bed and an array of sand-wiches and fruit drinks. When his escort came back to the interrogation room he sat himself down at the table, facing the lieutenant, waiting for the same old questions.

'Anything new from the other ex-prisoners?'

'No sir. They all say much the same. Our fellow was routinely beaten up and was finally in solitary. During the time he was in solitary he was handed over by the Koreans to the Chinese. Another thing was that they think our guy was not infantry but maybe signals.'

'Has he talked to any of the others since they were released?'

'No.' He shrugged. 'If a guy's been handled by the Chinese they keep away from him. Classed him as a possible informer. But they said that the sessions he had with the Chinese lasted four or five hours at a time. He definitely got the full treatment.' He paused. 'I don't think we'll get any more from him. Four sessions and not a word from him. And he wasn't with us at all. He's a very sick guy.'

The three of them sat around the table in the US Army HQ in Seoul. Grimmett was in charge and was moving them briskly through the items that needed an immediate decision. He reached for the next folio from the small pile of papers to his right on the table.

'RP7094.' He looked around the others. 'You both read it.'

When they both nodded Grimmett leaned back in his chair. 'What do we do, Frank?'

'As you see from the doctor's report the guy will be physically OK in six months or so provided he gets food and rest. But right now he's just a zombie. No responses to anything. Bearing in mind what we already know about what the Chinese got up to with prisoners, it's my opinion that this guy has been hypnotised or brainwashed with drugs.'

'So what're you gonna do with him?'

'I'll hand him over to our medics who know about hypnosis and see how they go.'

'And meantime, who is the poor bastard?'

'He's just RP7094.'

'For Chrissake, Frank. He's a soldier. What else can we do for him?'

For a few moments Frank was silent. 'I'd better lay it on the line for you.' He paused a long time as if he was working out how to say what he had to say. He looked across at Grimmett and said quietly. 'This guy's gone, Timmy. He's left us.' He paused again. 'And in my humble opinion he ain't ever coming back.'

Chapter Two

———————•———————

The Korean armistice was signed on July 27, 1953. After 37 months of bloodshed and 2,000,000 dead, 80 per cent of them civilians and 54,000 of them Americans, South Korea returned to more or less its original status. Syngman Rhee had gained 2,350 square miles of territory as against Kim Il Sing's 850 square miles. The United Nations had not even succeeded in establishing a reliable inspection system to prevent the North Koreans from launching another attack.

A month after the signing of the armistice, PFC Joe Maguire was sitting in a three-ton truck with a canvas covering, with ten US soldiers who had been taken prisoner by the North Koreans and released as part of the armistice deal. He was in charge of the party, assisted by a driver, and he had found it strange that he had been ordered to be armed all the time. As the truck bounced and bumped on the journey to Seoul, he found his charges subdued and he knew that not one of them was capable of any kind of resistance. So why the hell should they be treated more like prisoners than US soldiers released from a prison-cage? But there was no rejoicing among his passengers. They barely spoke, and sat on the two long metal benches as inert as rag-dolls. When he spoke to them they didn't respond, when he looked at them they closed their eyes, and when he offered them a drink or a Hershey bar they flinched from his outstretched hand as if he were about to strike them.

On arrival at the camp outside Seoul he had been angry to see the way the men were treated. When he complained he was told by an officer that a lot of returned prisoners had been indoctrinated by the N. Korean Communists and were not to be trusted. He was sufficiently incensed to ask for an interview with the Camp Commandant.

Captain Hagler looked at him as the orderly room sergeant stood him at ease and snatched his cap off and then the Captain pointed to the folding wooden chair.

'I understand you've got a complaint. What is it?'

'The returned prisoners in my charge are sick men and they're treated like enemy prisoners. Why, sir?'

'They'll be sorted out in due course, soldier, when they've been interrogated. They problem is they won't talk. We need to know why not. What are they hiding?'

'I can tell you why they won't talk, sir.'

'OK. Tell me.'

'Because they've been beaten up. They've got bruises all over them. They're scared. When they talked they were beaten up.'

'Good soldiers don't get taken prisoner.'

'Good leaders don't send men to fight with their hands tied behind their backs.'

Capt. Hagler raised his eyebrows and nodded to the sergeant who said, 'On your way, soldier. Move it.'

Capt. Hagler scribbled Maguire's name, and number, on his field service pad. Later he sent a note to the unit's security officer giving brief details of the interview and suggesting that PFC Maguire should be registered as a security risk for the future.

Maguire had been left to take his charges down to the port of Pusan from where they were being shipped back to the USA for interrogation. It was a long and tiring journey by army trucks and took several days. During the night-time stop-overs, Maguire treated his sad crew with the respect he genuinely felt for them as fellow soldiers who had been outgunned and outnumbered. He saw that they had full army rations and bought items they needed at the PK shacks on the route. A few of them actually responded but they were all too apprehensive to make any real contact. When they assembled on the quayside, waiting for Movement Control to assign them their berths on the troopship, Maguire had insisted that they had the same facilities and treatment as other troops. Another unfavourable report on PFC Maguire went back to his unit's CO. It was filed without being read and six months later Joe Maguire was promoted to sergeant. He had been sent on a staff course and had done well and it was on that course that he was told to report to Room Number 390 in the Pentagon building. The plate on the door said Colonel Swenson. He'd knocked on the door and a voice told him to go in. The man at the desk in the large room nodded to the chair facing him.

'Sit down, sergeant.' He looked intently at Maguire and then said quietly, 'I've been hoping to contact you for a long time.' He shrugged. 'But you already know how our paperwork on Korea was a complete mess.' He paused. 'Have you any idea why I wanted to contact you?'

'No, sir. I'm afraid not.'

'Before we talk about that, I'd like to ask you something.' He paused. 'What made you join the army, sergeant? You weren't drafted according to the records.'

Maguire smiled. 'I've often asked myself that.' He shrugged. 'To be honest I have to say I don't know why. I guess it was a mixture of wanting to be away from my safe life at home. Wanting some adventure. And I saw it as giving me a kind of status.'

'No political feelings?'

'No. Politics doesn't interest me.'

'Why not?'

Maguire shrugged. 'Politicians don't do anything. My grandfather always used to say that put the whole of Congress together and between them they couldn't make a henhouse. Farmers and manufacturers have to produce things people will buy. To me politicians just talk but take no risks and don't produce a damn thing.'

For a few moments the colonel looked away towards the windows and then, turning to Maguire he said. 'D'you remember the first group of released US PWs that you escorted down to Pusan?'

Maguire smiled. 'I certainly do. I got a black mark on my file.'

'Actually you got another black mark which you weren't told about from Movement Control at Pusan.' He paused. 'I found out a lot about you before I was able to trace where you were.' He paused and looked across at Maguire. 'My son was one of those returned PWs and he told me a lot about you. He was eventually discharged from the army but not until the people who interrogated him had wiped out the last bit of his self-esteem and the last of his pride in being an American. But you and your attitude had been a shining example of the other face of the United States.' He paused. 'So let me say on his behalf and on behalf of my family how much we appreciate that you cared enough to try and give those young men a square deal.'

For a moment Maguire was silent and then he said, 'Most soldiers would have had the same attitude as I had. But I'm very pleased if it helped your son adjust back to a more normal life. He shouldn't have been in Korea. None of us should. It was politicians again. They just threw us on the scrap-heap.'

'Are you going to stay in the army?'

'I haven't decided. I'm just not sure which way to go.'

'I want to suggest that the army could use young men like you. They need people who have minds of their own.' He paused. 'I've discussed it with other senior officers and I want to suggest that you are promoted to second-lieutenant and go for a six-month course at a training school. After that we have several appointments that might suit you.'

'I'm very flattered, sir, but are you sure that you aren't seeing more in me than is really there?'

'I'll tell you something, sergeant. Whether you take my advice and suggestion or you go off back to civilian life, you're going to be a success. Like it or not you've got qualities that this country is going to need more and more in the future.'

'Can I think about it, sir?'

'Of course. How long do you need?'

'Can I contact you tomorrow?'

'OK. Let's say this time tomorrow.' He paused. 'And let me say again – thanks for sticking up for my son and the others.'

Chapter Three

Lieutenant-colonel Maguire stood in the embassy compound watching the helicopters lining up to land on the embassy roof. Despite the inevitability of what was happening he still found it unbelievable. People shoving and screaming as they reached for the chopper's landing skids, trying to board the plane before it had landed. It was April 30, 1975, a Wednesday. There would only be four more transport flights and most of the passengers would be American civilians. The US Marines would see to that.

He felt a mixture of anger and shame, 40,000 American servicemen had died in Vietnam and more than 300,000 wounded. Nearly 200,000 South Vietnamese troops had died. For him the politicians were to blame. The United States had lost again. Lost not just an unnecessary war but had ended up by deserting an ally and leaving them to their fate.

The Jeep with his driver drove him to his pick-up point where the Sikorsky was taking on the last of the US embassy senior staff and the army and marine officers who were to be ferried to the aircraft carrier lying five miles out to sea.

It was a week later when President Ford made a speech declaring the end of the Vietnam Era and the termination of veterans' benefits. Despite the torrent of politicians' words, the stark facts excluded argument. Hundreds of thousands of Americans had been killed or maimed, seven million tons of bombs had been dropped and 141 billion dollars had been spent. When President Ford pleaded for national amnesia about Vietnam, only one public figure protested, saying 'My brother-in-law wakes up every day without his legs. How can he forget?'

Maguire had stayed on in the army for another year before he decided that he'd had enough. With the approval of his father he took three years out to take a law degree. When he joined the family practice as a partner he had tended to specialise in acting for ex-servicemen who felt they had not had a fair deal from the army. There were a lot of them about. He saw Swenson from time to time when he had business in Washington so he wasn't surprised when Swenson had phoned to ask if it was possible for him to come to Washington for a couple of days. All tabs would be picked up by the government. They had fixed a date and Swenson had booked him in to the Park Hyatt. Swenson had met him at Dulles and driven him to book in at the hotel. In the coffee room after the usual pleasantries, Swenson had said, 'Would you mind if we worked on something this evening?'

Maguire shrugged. 'Whatever you want suits me.'

'We've got a problem, Joe. We're hoping you could help us solve it.'

'Who's we?'

'The army, the CIA, the Treasury and State.'

Maguire laughed. 'And you think I could solve some problem that that lot can't solve themselves?'

'Part of the problem is that there are several solutions but none of the parties agree which one it should be.'

Maguire shrugged and smiled. 'Tell me more.'

'Before I do that I want you to have a look at some photographs and some film clips.' He paused. 'Are you ready to go?'

'Yeah.'

As Swenson pulled into the car-park at the CIA's Langley HQ, Maguire noticed that Swenson appeared to have his own parking slot with his initials on a white wooden board. Personal slots at Langley were few and far between. Especially for retired US Army generals.

They had ended up in an office on the fourth floor that adjoined a small projection room.

Swenson pointed to the chairs on one side of a long table. 'Make yourself comfortable.'

When Maguire was seated Swenson took a photograph from a folder and slid it across for Maguire to look at.

It was just a face. The face of a man in his fifties. Bald at the front but shaggy eyebrows, deep folds from each side of the nose to the corner of the mouth, strange staring eyes and a mouth that looked grimly aggressive. The second photograph that Swenson shoved across was the same man but this time the eyes and the mouth were relaxed and smiling.

When Maguire had pushed the photographs aside, Swenson said, 'Do you recognise that man?'

'No. Should I?'

'Well you've spent several days with him but it was a long time ago.'

'What's his name?'

'Lampard. Hugo Lampard.'

'What's he do?'

'Nothing full-time. He has to spend a lot of his time having medical treatment.'

'For what?'

Swenson pursed his lips and frowned for a moment and then said, 'We don't rightly know but it goes under the heading of random mental instability.' He paused. 'We could be more specific when you've met him and seen a demonstration of the problem.'

'Sounds very complicated. You said that I spent some time with him way back, when was this?'

For a few moments Swenson was silent and then he said quietly, 'That man was one of the released US prisoners that you took down to Pusan. He's the same age as you despite his appearance. Both photographs were taken on the same day. The smiling one was the normal one. The other shows the man under hypnosis.'

'Why is he being hypnotised?'

'He'd been hypnotised by the North Koreans while he was a prisoner and because he was returned with the others he was left in a kind of limbo. Under hypnosis but not knowing what he was supposed to be or to do. We've hypnotised him ourselves to try and get him free of the original hypnosis but it hasn't worked. It seems to make him worse.' He paused. 'Seemingly quite randomly he reacts to the original hypnosis and it makes him violent and unstable. We have to keep him under permanent observation. When he's normal he's quite pleasant and we keep him occupied as a librarian. He's kept in a medical centre in the country.'

'You think he might remember me?'

'No. I doubt it. The problem is that we have no legal grounds for holding him and no government department will take responsibility for his upkeep.'

'So why not tell them the truth? Surely it's the Pentagon's responsibility to give him the help he needs.'

'Unfortunately we can't do that, because we are using hypnosis on people ourselves. It's a CIA project that is top secret. The Pentagon choose not to believe our story and we're not willing to show him to outsiders when he's in one of his breakdowns.'

'So where do I come in?'

'We want to show you what he's like when he's unstable, so that you've actually seen it yourself. You're an ex-officer. A much respected one. And you're a lawyer who is experienced in making claims against the Pentagon on behalf of veterans who have been left incapacitated. We think that they might believe what you tell them, if necessary under oath, and with the veiled threat that you are considering bringing a case against them.'

'Would the veiled threat be for real or just a bluff?'

'That would be up to you. The Pentagon wouldn't like it but the CIA can bring enough pressure on the Pentagon to make them go along with it. If that's how they want to play it.'

'So why don't the CIA put pressure on the army without my involvement?'

'They refuse to get involved in having to give evidence about hypnotism unless they're forced to by a court.' He paused. 'They can't afford to go public about our own mind-control operations.'

Maguire shook his head slowly. 'Do we really have to mess around in that sort of thing?' He paused. 'And what sort of case in law could a lawyer make in these circumstances?'

'I've had a short film put together to show you why the CIA are involved with mind-control. It takes about an hour. I could get us some sandwiches from the restaurant if you're hungry.'

Maguire shrugged. 'Let's eat when I've seen the film.'

'OK. I'll lead the way. The projector is already set up. Take a chair by the projector and I'll switch the lights out. I'll use the remote control.'

What Swenson had described as a film was actually a series of single shots with comments from Swenson.

There were shots of four men playing cards. One of them was a large man in a grubby-looking singlet with every inch of his visible body covered with elaborate tattoos. The artwork varied from flying angels to naked girls and elaborate constructions of baskets of fruit and flowers.

'The guy with the tattoos is the main drive of a group of crazies who get their kicks from destroying government buildings. He doesn't know it but he keeps the CIA and the FBI informed on what they are currently up to.'

'Why should he do that?'

'He was having a course of dental treatment and one of the CIA groups fixed for him to be hypnotised when he was having an abscess removed. He's been one of ours ever since.' He paused. 'Now this guy walking in the street towards the camera is a Hungarian with Press documentation. He's in the hypnosis programme and he keeps us up to date on what Moscow and Budapest are looking for. He's not aware of the hypnosis. He uses a sauna regularly and we do our bit there. Here's a few shots of him with contacts.

'Now this one is the current major item. He's a senior CIA officer. He's head of the Soviet section based in this building and he's selling information to his Moscow friends for hard cash. We're letting him go on his weary way until we've built up a picture of all his Washington contacts. He's very time-consuming because we have to create a fair amount of phony information for him to pass on and keep the top secret stuff away from his office.'

'Is he hypnotised?'

'He had a benign brain tumour and went in dock for an operation. He's got a very small gizmo planted in his head and we use that. I don't know how but it's worked for six months or so.'

Swenson switched on the room lights and turned to Maguire. 'Tomorrow I'll arrange for you to see our friend Lampard. Normal and under hypnosis.' Swenson stood up and stretched his arms. 'Let's go back to your hotel and eat.'

When they had got to the coffee, Swenson said, 'What happened with you and Carole?'

Maguire shrugged. 'If I say that nothing happened,

nobody would believe me. But that's how it was.' He paused. 'We married too young and the timing was all wrong. I'd survived the shambles of Korea and I'd been promoted. Sounds pretty good. And it was. Until those bloody politicians got us into Vietnam. First of all we hardly saw one another. I was constantly away and when I was on leave it didn't work. She was a good girl but she was the girl next-door and I didn't like next-door any longer. What I was doing in the army seemed more pressing and more important than what was going on in Wichita Falls, Texas. When the chopper got me back to the aircraft carrier I got a bundle of mail and the divorce papers were among the mail. There was no ill-feeling on either side. We met and talked and it was obviously all over so far as she was concerned. And if I'm totally honest I didn't feel involved.' He shrugged. 'I was just an observer. A couple of years later she married a local fellow – not a service guy. Decent chap. Nothing wrong with him and he was home by six every night.' He sighed. 'I guess I wasn't cut out for married life.' Maguire leaned back in his seat as if he'd just given evidence to a court.

'You got anyone special these days?'

Maguire shook his head slowly. 'If they're bright and pretty they aren't going to put up with my life. I may be a lawyer now but old habits die hard.'

'How about I pick you up here tomorrow at nine?'

'OK with me.'

'Just to go over the situation again. This guy Lampard was hypnotised by the Koreans when he was a prisoner. It seems he was in hypnosis when they stuck him in with the others you took over. He was in a very depressed state but so were many of them. In ignorance of the background our people hypnotised him and it became obvious that we were putting one hypnosis on another. We had no way to cancel out the first hypnosis and from time to time he had mental crack-ups. Sometimes under our hypnosis these crack-ups are induced and he's under the original hypnosis but with us not knowing how to get him back to his original state. What you'll see tomorrow is Lampard normal, Lampard under our hypnosis and Lampard suffering a break-through of the Korean hypnosis. All we can do is get him back in our box before he completely succumbs.'

'Any clues as to why he breaks down?'

'No. They've checked and tried, but nothing. And our guys know more about mind-control than anyone in the field.'

Chapter Four

Swenson had introduced Maguire to the psychiatrist responsible for Lampard's case. Dr Rudkin didn't fit Maguire's idea of what a psychiatrist would look like. He was dressed in a brown sweater, baggy chinos and scruffy trainers. But he was easy-going and obviously experienced.

'I don't know exactly how he'll respond when he's under tension but don't panic if he gets aggressive. He calms down quickly. What you've got to remember is this, if he breaks down not under my control then it could be quite violent. And there's no way he can be under hypnosis from me twenty-four hours a day.' Rudkin looked at Swenson. 'Shall I bring him in and we'll see how it goes? Ask him about his library job and he'll be quite normal.'

When Rudkin came back with Lampard the man seemed quite normal. Smiling as they were introduced and shook hands.

Dr Rudkin pointed at a chair at the table.

'Sit down, Hugo. Smoke if you want to. We're off-limits in here as you know.'

'I'm OK, doc.' He smiled at Swenson and Maguire. 'It's always the quacks who break the house rules.'

Maguire said, 'Tell me about the library, Hugo.'

'Ah yes. The library. You must come over and see it. Twenty thousand items at the last count but we're going to put them on fiche or ROMs, they haven't yet decided.'

'What sort of categories do you cover?'

'Mainly medical. Every aspect of medicine. Some quite rare and some extremely valuable that are kept under special air-conditioning.'

Rudkin looked across the table at Lampard and said quietly. 'Let's you and me dream, Hugo. I'll count to five and then we dream.'

Lampard's face had lost all its animation as he listened to Rudkin counting slowly to five.

'Now dream, Hugo, until I count you back again and you'll forget all about dreams. Yes?'

Lampard sat still and then he spoke slowly with a slur.

'You never say what I'm to do . . . who is the one you call target . . . where can I find him . . .'

Then Lampard screamed, his head back, his mouth wide open, his tongue between his teeth.

'Calm down, Hugo . . . calm . . .'

Lampard stood up unsteadily, his chair toppling back to the floor then staggered to the desk, his arms sweeping the pads, pens and telephones crashing to the floor. Rudkin stood up a few feet away and said, 'We're done now. Hugo. No more dreams. When I count to five we shall not remember the dreams.

'One . . . two . . . three . . . four . . . five. That's it, Hugo. Wake up slowly.'

Rudkin's voice was soothing now and Lampard walked slowly back to his seat at the table but he didn't sit down.

'We're going to computerise the register and the software people will install it.' He looked white-faced at Rudkin. 'I don't feel too good, doc.'

Rudkin took his arm and looked at Maguire and Swenson as he led Lampard away.

'I'll just settle Hugo down and I'll be back.'

Swenson had poured them all a coffee from a Thermos jug and as they sat around the table Maguire turned to Rudkin.

'What we saw could happen without any hypnotism from you or anyone else?'

'Yes. It's totally unconnected and random.'

'Have you tried any cures by drugs or surgery?'

'We tried several drugs but they didn't work and there's no surgery that is suitable or effective.'

'Will it ever go away gradually?'

'No reason why it should. He's under a kind of half-cocked but permanent hypnosis.'

'Could he be employed somewhere else?'

'He'd end up in prison or in a mental hospital.'

'You're absolutely certain that he's not normally employable?'

'Absolutely sure.'

'Would you be prepared to give evidence in a court case for Lampard's compensation?'

'Not if I have to cover the CIA's mind-control operations.'

'What about testifying under security restrictions in
front of a Pentagon committee?'

'Maybe, but I'd want CIA cleared for any evidence I
give that isn't solely concerned with Lampard. He's not
one of our assets. Just an interesting accident.'

'What do you mean when you say he's not one of our
assets? What's an asset in this context?'

'It's the CIA's description of a person who we have
under mind-control conditions and who is used to carry
out CIA orders without being aware of it.'

'You mean they're not volunteers?'

'No. Not volunteers. Originally we used volunteers on
drug tests but we realised that a volunteer wasn't typical of
an asset. An asset has zero knowledge of what he does
under mind-control.'

Maguire turned to Swenson. 'That's all I need for the
moment. You and I need to talk.' He nodded to Rudkin.
'Thanks for your help, Doctor Rudkin.'

When Rudkin had left, Swenson said, 'What do you
think?'

'Well there's no doubt that Lampard deserves
heavy compensation. Just as much as if he'd lost a leg or
was incapacitated in any other way because of his war
service.'

'But?'

'The restrictions make a court case a loser. They'd have
to be persuaded some other way, the Pentagon.'

'You see the Pentagon as responsible?'

'Yes. No doubt of it. But they'd say it was an unavoidable hazard of war.'

'So what do we do?'

'Let me think about it.' He paused. 'Can you or the CIA give me a "to whoever it may concern" letter that allows me to talk to anyone I need to?'

'Yes. But not to investigate or discuss the CIA mind-control operation. That's right off the record.'

'Does their operation have a code name?'

'Yes. It's Operation MK Ultra.'

'What's the significance of the code name?'

'None. It was just sort of stuck on for convenience.'

'Does the operation have a structure?'

'Yes. But it's pretty loose because the kind of people who are used in the mind-control operation itself are mainly medics, not CIA or military. The assets are sometimes military and sometimes civilians.'

'Why are they referred to as assets? Seems a pretty cold attitude.'

'The mind-control is only the first phase. When an asset's mind is under control then other people in the CIA can use them for various activities.'

'Does it work?'

'It works very well.'

'Why are you involved in all this? You're US army, not CIA.'

'After Vietnam the CIA recruited me to act as a sort of top-level liaison with the Pentagon. Like you, I wanted a change so I accepted.' He shrugged. 'It has its problems but on the whole it works.' He paused. 'MK Ultra has its own budget, you can charge us your top rate.'

'It won't take long no matter which way it goes. I'd reckon about a week, but I'd have to stay in Washington most of the time.'

And it was then that Swenson was almost certain that Maguire would take the assignment.

'How about I leave you to it and we'll meet here again this evening?'

'Give me your mobile number and I'll call you when I've made a couple of calls and made up my mind one way or the other.'

'That's fine, Joe. If you need any help or information just call me. I'll be around all day.'

Maguire had spent several years battling with Pentagon lawyers and accountants and he was well-liked. He didn't behave as if he thought that Pentagon lawyers were trying to rob disabled ex-servicemen of their dues, but he was, all the same, a tough, competent negotiator. The man he needed to talk to was Kurt Heinz but he didn't have his phone number and he knew he wasn't in the telephone book. His number at the Pentagon was strictly private. Maguire sighed and phoned his office in Wichita Falls. He dialled the number they gave him. The phone was picked up on the third ring.

'Yeah,' the voice said noncommittally.

'It's Joe Maguire, Kurt. From Wichita Falls. We've met several times. I . . .'

Kurt Heinz laughed softly. 'You're a very modest man, Joe Maguire. You don't need to remind me who you are.

What can I do for you?'

'I'm in Washington for a couple of days, is there any chance I could have a few minutes of your time?'

'Is this a case of yours?'

'It depends on our chat.'

'I'm at the Pentagon, where are you?'

'At the Park Hotel.'

'How about you treat me to a decent cup of coffee and one of their lovely éclairs. I could be there in half an hour if the traffic's not worse than normal. OK?'

'I'm very grateful. I look forward to seeing you.'

They had talked for nearly an hour with Maguire giving only enough information to make the discussion useful.

'You say you've seen the guy in one of his distressed incidents. Why don't you just go through the normal moves in such a case?'

'Because for security reasons the people who have him don't want any publicity.'

'You're talking CIA aren't you?'

'Yes.' He paused. 'Let's say that the CIA are doing the same mind-control experiments but they dare not let it become public.'

'There'd be a lot of money involved, Joe. We couldn't avoid accounting for it.'

'Maybe we could make it an enhanced pension for disabilities suffered on active service in a war zone.'

'Who approached you on this?'

'General Swenson. He's retired but still employed by the Pentagon. I think he's their liaison with the CIA.'

'Does that mean that the Pentagon wouldn't put up any objections?'

'I'd guess so.'

'What rank was this guy?'

'Just a PFC.'

Heinz paused. 'Swenson. That name rings a bell. Must be getting on by now. Didn't he have a son in Korea? Lost a claim for disability from being beaten up or something in a Korean PW camp.' He paused. 'Or am I confusing him with someone else?'

'No, you're right, Kurt. The Pentagon refused the claim on the grounds that there was insufficient evidence that being beaten up was the basic cause of his breakdown, or even the main cause. The Pentagon paid all the legal costs but no damages.'

Heinz nodded. 'I remember reading that his son had hung himself two years later.'

'I didn't know any of that. I was still in the army at that time.'

'How many more of these cases are we going to get?'

'I'd guess this is the only one. It's special and a one-off because what happened to the guy has a close connection to a top-secret CIA operation. Without that connection it would be straightforward.'

'Apart the mental problems, how fit is he?'

'Apparently normal for his age.'

'And how old is he?'

'About fifty.'

'How much pension had you got in mind?'

'About forty thousand a year, paid monthly.'

'And that would be the end of it so far as the Pentagon is concerned?'

'Yes. But the CIA would owe you one.'

Kurt Heinz smiled and shrugged. 'God willing we never need one.' He sighed. 'OK, Joe. You and I can do the paperwork tomorrow. Payments monthly in arrears from the first of this month.'

They chatted for ten minutes or so and then Maguire walked Kurt Heinz back to the foyer and the official car that would take him back to the Pentagon.

As he sat with another cup of coffee, Maguire closed his eyes and thought about the talk with Kurt Heinz. Justice had been done and in fact no favours had been done. But he knew that if he had stuck to the formalities of the normal procedures the case would have been thrown out for lack of evidence because the CIA themselves wouldn't release the evidence. They claimed the protection of national security and Maguire realised that they were probably right in that claim. It would have involved a tangle of prejudices. By the CIA of the Pentagon and of the CIA by the Pentagon's lawyers. The only agreement they would have in the end would be that lawyers were paid to prevent justice being done.

Swenson had phoned and said he would be at the hotel in half an hour. He'd like to have a nice Scottish malt waiting for him.

He hung his jacket on the back of his chair as he settled at the low coffee table between them. He was holding his glass as he said, 'You look tired, Joe. Or are you wondering how to turn down the case without giving offence?'

Maguire smiled. 'I know you too well to be worried about offending you.' He leaned back in his chair. 'Let me tell you what I've done. I hope you approve.'

Swenson listened in disbelief and lowered his glass to the table without taking a drink. Ten minutes later he said, 'Tell me. Is what you've just outlined what you propose to do if you take on the case?'

'No, General. I've done it already. It's a deal, not a proposal.'

'How the hell did you get them to agree?'

'Just cutting out the bullshit and the pressures and telling the truth.' He paused. 'All the truth that needed to be told anyway. Enough for them to turn it down if they so chose.' He paused again. 'But you'd better make clear to your CIA people that they owe a big favour to a guy named Kurt Heinz, a senior lawyer at the Pentagon.'

'Were there any restrictions?'

'Two. That nobody would come back for more and that this was the only case where CIA security was used without investigation.'

'I still can't believe it, Joe. I'd reckoned on at least three months of hassle.' He shook his head. 'You're a genius.' He paused. 'Charge us on the case, not the time taken.'

'I don't want a fee. Just pick up my hotel and travel and that's all I want.'

'Why, Joe? You've done a wonderful job. You deserve a proper fee.'

'Forget it.' Maguire paused and said. 'I was sorry to learn about what happened with your boy. Kurt Heinz remembered his case. I'm sure it played a part in this business.'

Swenson looked towards the window and Maguire saw the tears brimming in the old man's eyes. Too choked to speak. Just thinking again of that figure hanging from the branch of the tree in the orchard.

Maguire had spent two hours the next day with Kurt Heinz and they completed the documentation. Swenson and Maguire had signed along with Kurt Heinz and another senior Pentagon lawyer. Maguire had taken the evening plane to Dallas Fort Worth and cadged a lift from a pilot friend back to Wichita Falls. The sun was just coming up as he walked across to the hangar where he had parked his car. The thing that Swenson had asked him to deal with had taken his mind back to those dreadful days in Korea and eventually in Vietnam. In a strange way it made him wonder if he didn't belong more in the army than in the law. Like most lay people he was not a fan of the CIA but now that he had had a glimpse of what they do and the world they operate in, he felt that at least they were doing their part in defending the country.

Chapter Five

The woman on the other side of the desk looked at Tony Rice.

'I've tried to explain, Mr Rice.' She paused. 'I can't put you down for consideration with all this information missing.'

'What is it you want?'

She sighed theatrically and leaned back in her chair.

'You've got two years missing from your CV. I've checked personally with the personnel guy at the army medical base where you were stationed.' She shrugged. 'No problem except that the army says you were discharged nearly two years ago and you say it was only a month ago.' She leaned forward. 'Have you got something you want to hide? There's no problem with the army, they confirm it was an honourable discharge at your own request.' She shrugged again. 'So what's the problem? If there's been some sort of mix-up, you'd better get it sorted out or you're going to have difficulty getting a job that needs a full CV and references.'

'Couldn't you sort it out after you've hired me?'

'Tony. It is Tony, isn't it? Look, I can't spend time doing what you should be doing. You'd better get a lawyer or somebody who can take up your case.' She shrugged. 'These things happen you know. You must have papers or something that shows what happened. It's these darn computers that cause all the trouble.'

It was Tony Rice's mother who spoke to the family doctor about him.

'He just sits around doing his jigsaw puzzles. He isn't well, doctor. I'm his mother and I know him. He's always been a bright boy and now he's in some world of his own. He needs to get a job to liven himself up.'

'Have a word with my receptionist on your way out, Mrs Rice. Make an appointment for your son to see me.'

The family doctor found Tony Rice to be in good shape physically but was concerned at his mental state. Unable to give any idea of what could be troubling him. He seemed as mentally confused as an elderly man would be, but with no physical grounds for his lethargy.

He wrote to the unit where Tony Rice had been employed to ask about his medical records and the unit's medical officer had written back to say that there had been no physical or mental problems. PFC Rice had done his job well and had left the army at his own request.

As a final move he had suggested that Rice should

contact the Veteran's Administration to see if they could help.

After the usual delays of any kind of officialdom, the report on the interview with Tony Rice landed on the desk of a man who had gone to the same school. He had talked to Rice for an hour and had been shocked at his condition. The VA agreed that it was worthwhile the VA man making direct contact with Rice's old unit in Arizona.

The officer who met with the VA official was polite and amiable but obviously trying to make sure that no blame was being cast on the US Army for Rice's condition.

'I think you've admitted that there is no evidence of PFC Rice having this condition when he was discharged.'

The VA man said sharply. 'You say "admitted". I haven't "admitted" anything. I'm only involved to see if the VA can improve things for PFC Rice.'

'My apologies. A careless use of the word. I should have said "agreed". That you agree that when he left here he was sound in wind and limb, as they say.'

'Yes. But it's his mental condition that is the problem.'

'I don't feel we can be held responsible for that. He was OK when he left this base.'

'Did you check the date on his discharge papers?'

'Yeah. He left the army about eighteen weeks ago. That's what his papers say.'

'How the hell can a guy lose a chunk out of his life and not know it?' He paused. 'Maybe it would help if I spoke to some of his work-mates when he was here.'

For the first time the VA man felt that there was something odd when the officer said, 'That would need the Commandant's permission. This is a high-security unit.'

'But you told me that Rice was only responsible for dispatching parcels already wrapped.'

'It still would need the CO's permission for you to interview members of our staff.' He looked at the VA man. 'Between you and me I suggest you leave things as they are. It may be to Rice's disadvantage to keep poking around in what is obviously just a misunderstanding on Rice's part.'

The VA man was incensed at the officer's attitude.

'In that case I'll have to get one of our lawyers take the matter up.'

'Tell me, pal. Why all the fuss about this guy? Is there something you aren't telling me?'

'No. But I'm beginning to wonder if there's something *you* aren't telling *me*.'

The officer stood up. 'I find that very offensive. I think we'd better leave it. I've told you the facts. If you doubt the facts that's too bad.' He held out his hand. 'I'll walk you to the guard-room and clear you through.'

Maybe if the officer who interviewed the man from the Veterans' Administration had known that the man with the grey hair and the ruddy complexion had been a captain in Special Forces before retiring to make a fortune in lumber and giving his spare time to the VA, he would have been a little more cautious in his attitude. The meeting had been secretly taped and the officer's superiors had not been impressed. He had been posted to a medical unit in Germany two days after the meeting. All Rice's contacts at the base had been moved to other army medical units.

Captain (Retd.) Crosby had spent many long hours listening to suspect stories of some incident or complex scenario and he had an instinct for knowing when the lying began. He couldn't have described how it worked for he didn't know. It wasn't the expression on a man's face or a hesitation in his speech, nor a man's appearance and demeanour. Some of the shrewdest liars were absolutely charming. It was their business.

Crosby's assessment of the medico was that he was lying from the start with a well-prepared story and the feeling that it was all very simple. He didn't feel that his lies were really lies. They'd been concocted and approved by others above him. He was just carrying out orders. But the story was so simple and so unimportant. Just a mild precaution, not a major deception, and no account had been taken of what attitude to adopt if there was any resistance to the story.

So why was talking to Rice's old work-mates so important that the lies became obvious? You didn't need to be an experienced interrogator to recognise the panic when the story was queried. If it had been almost any other of the Veterans' Administration's staff the story would almost certainly have been accepted. But not Captain (Retd.) Crosby. But was it worth kicking up a stink about it? He decided that it was and he'd passed his notes and report to Legal and they had passed them on to Joe Maguire for his opinion.

At first reading Joe Maguire had been doubtful about

pressing the case. What was the man chasing? Was he, in fact, chasing anything? If his CV was showing some ridiculous administrative discrepancy, why didn't he take a job where a CV was not required? And why was the man's mother the instigator, not the man himself? He checked the address. Little Rock. Maguire reckoned that a couple of days out of Houston and Wichita Falls might do him good.

Joe Maguire's father had set up a law office in Houston partly because it would be highly profitable and partly to give his son a reason to be in charge of his own operation away from the routine of Wichita Falls. Joe Maguire put a note in his diary to interview Tony Rice when he visited a client in Little Rock in two weeks' time.

Chapter Six

Joe Maguire had booked himself into the Carriage House Bed and Breakfast. There were only two guest rooms but there was peace and quiet and the whole atmosphere combined the sophisticated and the homespun that were Little Rock's characteristics.

He had spent the morning and lunch-time with his client and they had ended up reviewing their efforts taking afternoon tea in the courtyard of the Carriage House.

It had been a long-drawn-out case concerning land rights and development rights. He had won his case with the State without leaving a residue of resentment in the State House. It concerned the riparian rights of the land on the banks of the Arkansas River and the State had accepted Joe Maguire's personal guarantee that the land would not be developed into any kind of amusement park. In fact, Maguire's client intended setting up a centre for the visual arts covering photography, cinematography, painting and sculpture. The centre would be named after his client's wife.

As his client, Karl Ober, leaned back in his wicker armchair, he smiled at Maguire.

'I don't see you as part of this old-world atmosphere, Joe. Why here?'

Maguire shrugged. 'I don't see why not.' He waved his hands. 'This is my America. Decent people living decent lives. Not screwing everyone for the last cent, just earning a decent living.'

Ober smiled. 'You should be in politics, Joe.'

'No way. Why me?'

Karl Ober laughed at the sight of the genuine indignation on his lawyer's face. Then, his face serious now, he said, 'The people of this country are sick of politicians. All of them. They hate them. Democrats and Republicans alike. They see them as hypocrites and crooks. It used to be used-car salesmen that nobody trusted. These days it's politicians.' He paused. 'Don't tell me you don't see 'em in the courts every day. Touting for a land reclamation grant, or a government contract for a company they get a kick-back from. Congress goes on about terrible human abuses in some country, but you can bet your dollar that there'll always be a group of politicians who claim that the offenders are our biggest customer for something or other and the atrocities are figments of the opposition's imagination.' He sighed and shrugged. 'You don't need telling, Joe. You know as well as I do what it's like.'

'Sure I know. But what I know doesn't tempt me to get mixed up with those games.'

'You're a fine attorney, Joe. But the rest of your talents are being wasted.'

'What talents for God's sake?'

'You were a great sportsman and many people said you could have been a pro. You've got a reputation as an exceptionally talented soldier. You work on what amounts to a *pro bono* basis for people who are up against the State but with no resources. You live a calm, modest life and you're financially independent.'

'There are hundreds of men with similar credentials and better in many cases.' He paused. 'Can you imagine me sitting on some committee trading my vote for some piddling party deal? No way.'

Ober smiled. 'What you just said is why I think you should be in the Capitol.'

And that's how the conversation had ended. And Joe Maguire had been mildly resentful at being judged as a potential politician.

The same evening Maguire had called at the home of his Vet client. He had talked with his mother and then alone in Tony Rice's small bedroom.

What he had learned disturbed him but what disturbed him even more was that look in the man's eyes. A look he had seen once before at his visit to Swenson in the CIA offices in Langley. The look of a man whose mind was somewhere far away.

Back at his office he had reached for the phone to put a call in to Swenson but at the last moment he decided against it. He wasn't sure why. Or at least he wouldn't admit to himself why he didn't make the call.

He spent much of his spare time trawling through the records of his time as a US Army trouble-shooter. He could remember the old days very well but he couldn't remember the guy's name except for the fact that it was Polish or Czech. Almost ten days had gone by when he saw the name in a different context. Sig Levinski's name came up in the credits at the end of a TV film as a stunt-man. It wasn't the same man but it was the same name and a few hours research gave him an address and a telephone number. A few years old but worth trying. The address was a University in Chicago and a phone call confirmed that Dr Sigmund Levinski was still on the medical faculty but was now a professor.

Maguire had remembered the Army doctor, not much older than he was, who had talked to him about the effects of stress on servicemen who had witnessed or taken part in incidents that had literally shocked them. He had said that he was experimenting with hypnosis as a cure for trauma. Maguire had been impressed by Levinski's anger about the Army doing so little to help its trauma victims.

And Levinski remembered the young and energetic colonel who had confronted him back in the bad old days. The grim days for army men when the disastrous war in Vietnam was in its final months. Men with nightmares that wouldn't go away.

Maguire had talked on the phone to Levinski for half an hour but was hampered by the fact that he couldn't mention the episode at the Pentagon. But Levinski was interested and agreed to fly down to meet Maguire in Dallas.

*

Levinski was a quiet, thoughtful man and he'd listened to all that Maguire had to say and asked a number of questions.

'One last thing, Joe. What made you think that this guy had been hypnotised at some time?'

Maguire was silent for a few moments and then said. 'I can't give you any details but he had a funny look about him and I'd seen that look before, on the face of a man whose hypnotism had gone wrong somehow. I don't understand the details.'

'And you and the Vets want me to sort your guy out and get him going again?'

Maguire laughed. 'I guess that's about it.' He paused. 'We'd pay of course, and expenses.'

'We'll see. If it's interesting and I'm able to publish it the University might be willing to fund it.' He paused. 'When can we see your guy?'

On the way back from Little Rock, Levinski said quietly. 'Your fellow has been hypnotised and hasn't been brought back properly to his normal state. The missing period covers when he was being used by somebody and he doesn't remember anything about it. I suspect he had no idea that he was being controlled under hypnosis.'

'What can be done to put him back to normal?'

'If I was doing it I'd hypnotise him and get him to talk about what he was doing in that missing time. Then clear him properly of all hypnotic controls.' He paused. 'But I suspect that neither your people nor the guy himself would like what we learned.'

'Why?'

'Because I suspect that what he was doing was outside the law.'

'What law?'

'Heaven alone knows, Joe. Best not to anticipate.'

'Would you do it if the Vets fund it?'

'I guess so. It's too intriguing to back away from.'

'How long is it likely to take?'

'The hypnosis is comparatively simple. The rest of the time depends on what he's been doing under the previous hypnosis.' He paused. 'It ain't gonna be good news that's for sure.'

'Why do you say that?'

'You don't hypnotise somebody over two years just for the hell of it.'

'I'll have to discuss it with my Vet's committee and I'll get in touch.'

'If they give you the go-ahead, I'll talk to the faculty about funding.'

After a couple of days of thought, Maguire decided that he would go ahead without consulting the committee. They were well funded and if there were going to be problems from the revelations he wanted to know before he put the details to the committee.

When he phoned Levinski the professor had already arranged for the faculty to bear any costs involved. The only restriction was that if the end result was sufficiently interesting to warrant publication in a medical journal, it would be under Levinski's and the faculty's names. The details and identity of the subject would remain strictly anonymous no matter what the result might be.

It had been two weeks before Levinski contacted Maguire again and he sounded cautious and almost unfriendly as he told Maguire that he would need two more weeks before he could report his findings. When Maguire had asked how the operation was going in general Levinski had said that when he was ready to report it would need to be on a person-to-person basis and not on the telephone or in writing. There was a distinct air of disapproval in Levinski's attitude.

When Levinski eventually phoned him it was to arrange a meeting and it was agreed that they would meet that coming weekend in Dallas.

Levinski had said that they would need two days and Maguire booked them both in at the Hyatt Regency.

Chapter Seven

Levinski had insisted that they talked only in their rooms and they used Levinski's room for their first meeting. Maguire had poured coffee for them both and set the mugs down on the low table between them where he had put his papers.

'You seemed a bit frosty on the phone, Siggy. Are you regretting getting involved in this thing?'

Levinski smiled rather wanly. 'I'm in two minds about it. Scientifically it's interesting. In every other way it disgusts me. But I apologise if I was frosty. What disgusts me will, I suspect, disgust you just as much. And at the end of it all you've got a tough decision to make. I don't envy you that dilemma.' He paused. 'Let me give you a run-down on our friend Tony Rice. OK?'

'However you want, my friend. Go ahead.'

'It started nearly five years ago. He had an appointment with an army dentist for dealing with a very painful abscess on a wisdom tooth. Unfortunately for him some zombie from the CIA was looking for somebody who could be anaesthetised without knowing it, and friend Rice was hypnotised as he came out of the anaesthetic. From that point on he was controlled by the CIA man and used in an experimental operation called MK Ultra.' Levinski paused and took a photograph from his file and handed it to Maguire. 'What do you make of that?'

'It looks like a tattoo on a man's wrist. A number of some sort.'

'The tattoo says EA 1729. Does that mean anything to you?'

'No, I'm afraid not.'

'It's a CIA code. The code the CIA use for LSD – lysergic acid diethylamide. It indicates that that person has been given LSD. The code is used solely by a highly secret section of the CIA. They wanted to find out if using LSD made a subject easier to control. Particularly when it was used in conjunction with hypnosis.' Levinski paused. 'Rice went back to his unit for three days – under hypnosis. During that time the formalities were completed for his discharge. He didn't contact his family and he went with his CIA controller to a CIA safe-house in the San Francisco area. He was based there for the next two years but he spent most of his time in Berlin and Warsaw. When he was under hypnosis he was called Max.'

'What was he doing in Berlin?'

'He killed people his controller told him to kill. But I remind you that he didn't know what he did under hypnosis. His cover was that he was a clerk at an import/export company. It was owned by the CIA.'

'Who were the people he killed?'

'Four Russians, six East Germans, one West German.

At least three Americans.' He paused. 'There were others, mainly Americans, in Somalia and Kenya.'

'When did it end?'

'A few months ago.'

'Why did it end?'

'Because Rice's controller was killed in a car accident . . .' he shrugged '. . . so far as I can tell, a genuine accident. Rice was under hypnosis at the time and nobody knew that he was being used in a hypnosis programme.' He paused. 'I've de-hypnotised him. But he doesn't know what he did and he doesn't know that he was hypnotised, nor that he's talked to me about those times or that I've hypnotised and de-hypnotised him. As near as he can be he's back to normal.'

'D'you have any evidence of all this?'

Levinski shook his head slowly as if in despair. 'Joe, we're not in court or even thinking of courts.' He paused. 'And from what I've learned the past few weeks, I can tell you, you wouldn't get near a court.'

'Why not?'

'Because another specimen like Max would wipe you out.' He paused. 'I've done hour after hour of taping my dealings with your chap Rice and I've destroyed it all apart from about ten minutes of extracts and when I've played them to you they too will go in the furnace. We're dealing with a different world here, Joe. A world with no laws, no justice and no restraints. If somebody gets in the way or acts against you – no problem – you kill 'em.'

'But as of now Rice won't remember anything about being hypnotised or the things that he did under hypnosis.'

'Right. So far as Rice is concerned none of it ever happened.'

'And he'll be able to get a job?'

'Yes. So long as your pals in the Pentagon have really straightened out Rice's records like you told them so that there's no missing time.'

For long moments Maguire was silent and then, looking across at Levinski, he said, 'It's gonna take me some time to absorb all this. Can we talk again tomorrow?'

'You'd better hear the taped extracts. They're the crux of the whole nightmare.'

Maguire sat listening to the slowly unwinding tape in the Sony Walkman and heard Rice being de-briefed after he had killed a man outside a club in one of the streets off the Ku-damm in Berlin. It was like a man describing having delivered a parcel. Faintly amused at his exploit but eager for approval. Maguire heard Rice being brought back from his hypnotic state and told to forget everything that had been done and said. He heard him become Tony Rice again, the voice less forced and talking about the book-keeping work that he did for the small import/export company that he seemed to be working for.

When he was back in his own room and undressing for bed, Maguire sat for a few moments watching the end of the CBS news on TV. He realised that he wasn't really shocked. Not like Levinski was. More surprised at what went on that was so well-hidden. But for him, he instinctively accepted that if these things were being done it was because there was a war. An underground war and the men who were involved were doing what had to be done to protect the country. Tony Rice could go back to Little Rock and get a job with his new documentation and have no idea of how he had been used. Was he *used* or exploited, and how many more Tony Rices were there doing the CIA's dirty work around the world? And who was he, Joe Maguire, to sit in judgment on men and women who were operating against ruthless opponents who had no scruples in their attempts to bring down the United States? But his lawyer's mind couldn't prevent him from the thought that if he did nothing he was an accessory to what was being done.

They had met for breakfast and Levinski deliberately left the subject of Tony Rice for Maguire to raise. They were on the second cups of coffee when Maguire said quietly, 'A couple of questions, Siggy, OK?'

'Go ahead.'

'Am I correct in thinking that all Rice's documentation now coincides? No different dates, no discrepancies?'

'That's it. The whole episode is wiped from start to finish.' He half-smiled and shrugged. 'What tailors call a seamless repair.'

'No problems on that score for him?'

'No problems, period.'

'My next question is about the CIA man who used and controlled Rice. Have you any idea who he was and who his superior was?'

'When I had hypnotised him I had to talk as if I knew everything that had been going on.' He paused. 'The only slight clue I got was that he referred several times to somebody he called Willard. I couldn't even tell whether it was a first-name or a family name. From the context it could have easily been a woman.'

'How much of this are you going to publish?'

'None. Absolutely none. I just want to write it off and forget it. And I've not kept the faculty informed.'

'How soon will he be able to fill in a CV and not cause a problem?'

'Right now. I checked this morning. It's all in place. Just tell him it was an admin mix-up.'

'Any grounds for claiming compensation for him?'

Levinski shrugged. 'All the grounds in the world but I strongly suggest you don't raise such an issue. Like I said, it wouldn't even get to court.'

'Did you check on the accident that killed the CIA operator?'

'No. Enough's enough, Joe.'

'I guess I ought to apologise for getting you involved in all this. I'm sorry.' He paused. 'Some people would have made a national scandal out of it.'

'Forget it. You didn't know what it was all about. And, if I'm totally honest, as a psychiatrist I found it — not, perhaps, fascinating, but incredibly informative.'

That was how they left it. Maguire had spoken on the phone to Tony Rice who sounded lively and energetic. A month later Maguire got a 'thank-you' letter from Rice who had been taken on as a telephonist at a local hospital.

Chapter Eight

Joe Maguire was not a connoisseur of good food and fine cooking, especially when they were part of a formal dinner or lunch. Joe Maguire ate only when he was hungry but on this particular night he had to attend the dinner because he was to be the guest speaker and the dinner was to celebrate the year's endeavours of the Veterans' Administration.

It was February when they asked him to be the speaker and nobody had borne in mind that although it was a long way ahead, it would be immediately after the elections and there would be a new president or, at least, a president elect.

On the night there had been the usual toasts and valedictory speeches, but when Joe Maguire was introduced the chairman went through the usual ritual of claiming that Joe Maguire needed no introduction and then launched into a litany of the high points of Joe's career as a professional soldier, a great sportsman and a lawyer who always remembered that the law and justice were not always the same thing.

Joe Maguire stood up and tossed a small notepad to one side.

'Ladies and gentlemen, I've just thrown away the notes for my so-called speech. I'm not an after-dinner speaker as some of you already know to your cost. There are other things, things that I find important, that I feel need saying. Out loud and in public. Things that affect this great country of ours.' He paused. 'But there's one thing I must say before I ramble on. We've got a new president standing in the wings after last week's elections. George Bush. And George Bush was a World War Two bomber pilot, and for me that's enough. I wish him well. During the time that he was Ronald Reagan's Vice-president military expenditure was increased and the Strategic Defence Initiation was launched. Those two knew what the world was all about and did something about it.'

Maguire waved down the clapping, took a deep breath and went on.

'The day after the election results were declared I was talking to a man about Ronald Reagan and George Bush. All he remembered about President Reagan was that he named the people in Hollywood who were active communists ready to use their influence and talents to benefit our foreign enemies. For George Bush, he didn't seem to remember that he was the youngest pilot in the US Navy when he joined and was later awarded the Distinguished Flying Cross and three Air Medals for his service in the Pacific. That conversation has been in my mind ever since.' Maguire sighed and looked around the faces in the room.

'I'm a member of a political party but I've no great

respect or love for politicians. Especially ours.' He paused. 'All over the world I see our country criticised to the point of insult. Our way of life, our efforts for equality are a constant source of criticism by people who purport to have only the interests of the poor at heart. If we're so bad, why do we have to spend millions of dollars every year to sort out the tens of thousands of people who are desperate to be allowed to live here? And if we are so selfish, why don't we just close the frontiers? – We can get by without the rest of the world.

'Why, when some thugs blow up one of our embassies or consulates, does the government of the country concerned do nothing to prevent such attacks or bring the criminals to justice?

'Not long ago Pan American Flight 103 was blown up in mid-air over Scotland on its way to New York. The latest figures indicate that at least two hundred and fifty people lost their lives – most of them Americans. There's no doubt who made and planted the bomb that blew up Flight 103. It was the Libyans. Libyan terrorists acting on the orders of Gaddafi.' He raised his voice. 'But we're not supposed to say it out loud. It isn't diplomatic. The diplomats have got to work out if we need Libyan oil. I can tell the ambassadors to give Gaddafi a message. We don't need his oil. He can keep it and let any country that buys Libyan oil from this time on know that it is dealing with murderers and we shall do our best to stop them. Don't tell me we should leave it to the United Nations to see justice done. Forget it. The UN has never acted on our behalf since it was founded. When they want money for that edifice in New York then we're the good guys, but when our interests are threatened or our citizens abused and attacked we are cautioned to say nothing that might upset the other side.' He paused. 'And who do I mean by the other side? I mean the Soviet Union, Communist China and all those tin-pot Middle East terrorists who see us as easy targets because we never hit back.

'When there are natural disasters – floods, earthquakes, tornadoes, that destroy some overseas community, the first planes in with relief and help will be ours. But when the disasters are in the US of A then it's up to us to cope. Fair enough. We *will* cope and we are proud to be able to help others in distress.

'Time and time again I see on TV news hooligans in some country burning our flag, shouting threats and obscenities while another group from the same country is shown assembling at the White House for talks with our government officials, asking for financial help for their virtually bankrupt economies because the first package of finance is lying safely in Swiss banks and off-shore trusts. Maybe I'm crazy but this strikes me as Alice in Wonderland. We're told not to go on about it because it's all part of the diplomatic game. If it is – then to hell with the diplomatic game.

'And it's not just a question of physical violence. There are groups of people who work in more subtle ways to destroy the fabric of our society. We are told that it is wrong for our children to sing our national anthem or salute the Stars and Stripes. Others demand that the armed forces should accept homosexual recruits. And underneath it all we have the huge infrastructure of drugs. When we protest to the countries who are the source of millions of dollars worth of drugs we are told that growing drugs is the only thing their citizens can do to earn a living. We are apparently selfish in criticising them and defending our own people from the drug barons.'

Joe Maguire looked around the assembled people and said quietly, 'More and more we are being attacked by ruth-less terrorists, who blow up our public buildings and undermined our inheritance that was so hard-earned. I thought it was time to speak out, to expose the diplomatic hog-wash and to put down a marker for the rest of the world to see.' He paused. 'We seek no territory, no resources, no empire but we will defend all the way our constitution, and our chosen way of life. We wish no one ill. But beware. We mean to survive.' He paused. 'Thank you for listening. I guess I've gone on too long. Forgive me.'

Joe Maguire sat down and after a moment's strange silence his audience stood and applauded him for what seemed a long time. He looked uncomfortable.

General Swenson had been the guest of honour at the dinner and later Maguire took him to meet a number of local people from the political parties and from business.

There had been several favourable comments on Maguire's speech but it was obvious that Maguire was not prepared to involve himself in any further discussion. He had stayed for half an hour or so and had then left the group and walked through to the hotel entrance. He looked up at the night sky; he had made up a camp-bed in his office for the night and decided to walk.

It was after midnight but the streets were full of traffic and there were queues for taxis as the restaurants and theatre crowds began to call it a day. It was only a month from the Christmas break but the sky was clear and the air was warm.

At his office he chatted for a few minutes with the guard in the foyer who unlocked the doors to let him in. It seemed like the word had already got around about Maguire's speech. As he let himself into his office suite he realised that no matter that he'd announced his party-piece as just a chat, it had become a speech whether he liked it or not. It had needed saying but somebody else more important should have said it.

The four men with Swenson were still talking when it began to get light and Roy Marr held up his hand.

'Let's go over it one more time. OK, Sam?'

'OK by me, Roy.'

'We all know the things that these creeps on selection committees go for.' He paused. 'First, is he a registered voter?'

'Yeah, he's been registered as a Republican for nigh on ten years but he plays no part in any politics.'

'Why not?'

Swenson smiled. 'Forgive me when I say he loathes all politicians irrespective of party.'

'Finances. Any money worries?'

'No. He's made several million and behind that is the family money.'

'Speculation?'

'Merrill, Lynch look after his money.'

'Army record?'

'It's in the CV I gave you. Ideal in every way.'

'Women? Sexual stuff?'

'No philandering when he was married. He's had a few relationships since then. No scandal. Nothing in any closets. Those I've met obviously liked him.'

'Prejudices?'

'Doesn't like politicians and diplomats and doesn't like abuse of authority.'

'Give us a fault. Anything.'

'A bit tight-fisted with money. Rather narrow outlook on the world in general.'

'What's that mean?'

Swenson smiled. 'An isolationist but wouldn't recognise the name. Let's just say he's an America First sort of guy.'

'So how are you going to get a fellow who hates *all* politicians to become a politician himself?'

'In this case we don't want him to indulge in the usual political games. We just want him to have the status. And the authority when it's needed. He'll take over my present role and he'll give us an impeccable image.'

It was Cooper, Congressman Cooper, who put the underlying question.

'How are the Democrats going to react to the idea of a Republican Senator no matter how popular he may be?'

Swenson looked across at Cooper and smiled. 'He'll stand as an Independent.'

'And Washington?'

'There's some kind of sweetie for anyone likely to be involved. Langley have all the strings attached to all the appropriate hooks. Once we get over the nomination we're virtually there.'

It went back to Roy Marr. 'Are you sure he'll be interested?'

'Pretty well. It covers all his bases. Armed forces, the law, the constitution, and above all he would be defending the country against all those things he just happened to talk about tonight.' He smiled. 'I guess it was last night.' He put his hands on the arms of his chair as if he were about to stand up, but he just said quietly, 'Do we press the button?'

'When?'

'I reckon we've got six months' work ahead. We should get him moving right away.'

Nobody disagreed although nobody said he agreed. But that was how politicians quietly put down their markers in case something didn't work. Nothing in writing and never any out-and-out commitments.

Maguire had picked up Swenson from the hotel next morning and driven him to the airport. There was a delay of half an hour and they went to the coffee-shop. As Maguire helped himself generously to sugar, Swenson said, 'We appreciated how you dealt with the Anthony Rice business. It was building up to be something of a scandal.'

Maguire looked sharply across at Swenson. 'How the hell did you know about that business? I didn't mention it to you.'

Swenson shrugged. 'It's what I'm there for, Joe. Just keeping an eye on things that could go wrong. Trying to put the Band-aid on before the infection spreads.'

'Is this the Pentagon?'

'No. But there are a lot of armed services connections.'

'So who do you operate for?'

Swenson smiled. 'Let's say I'm a consultant.'

'For whom?'

'For the CIA.' He paused. 'Maybe not so much a consultant as a trouble-shooter.'

'I'll have to watch what I say to you in future.'

'What you and I discuss together is just the two of us. I don't pass it on. And I don't use it.' He paused. 'They're calling my flight.' As he stood up he said, 'You're going to get a lot of calls about your speech last night.'

'It *was* a bit over the top.'

'Most people will agree with every word you said.' He paused. 'It needed saying.'

Swenson's forecast was right. Maguire had to take on a temporary secretary to deal with sorting out the telephone calls and the piles of letters that came in the next two weeks. The Republican organisation in Austin had sent him two more temporary assistants but he had been glad that he was involved in litigation in court that took him away from the turmoil in his office.

What made him uneasy was the constant flow of invitations to talk to a wide spectrum of organisations and an equally wide variety of social invitations. Despite what he had said in his speech to the Veterans' Administration, there were many invitations from politicians apparently anxious to talk to him.

When the incumbent Senior Senator, Billy Archer, found that he had to resign on grounds of ill-health,

Swenson's small but influential group swung into action as if it had all been planned months before. Which of course it had. It had taken a month longer than expected because the bank had not taken gladly to Billy Archer becoming Chairman of the Board.

It was autumn when Joe Maguire won a landslide victory over his only rival. The celebrations were limited to three days but oddly enough the reluctant candidate, now Senator Maguire, rather enjoyed his new status.

Chapter Nine

———————◆———————

The crash of glass breaking violently woke him and for a moment he had no idea where he was. Then he remembered. He was in a hotel and Jamieson was in the next room. Glass was still breaking and falling as he struggled into his bathrobe and hurried into the lounge. The ten-foot-high window was smashed and the curtains were blowing back into the room. He could hear the noise of the traffic in the street. Jamieson wasn't in his room and then the dreadful facts came into focus. He could hear police and ambulance sirens and he reached for the phone.

He dialled Frazier's home number and obviously roused him from his sleep.

'Frazier. Who the hell are you?'

'It's Goldman. Something's happened.'

'Can't it wait till tomorrow for God's sake?'

'It's Jamieson. He jumped out of the window.'

'Is he dead?'

'I don't know but I can hear police cars and ambulances.'

'What floor are you on?'

'I don't remember. Twenty-first or twenty-second.'

'Listen. When the police come you don't answer any questions. Tell 'em to get in touch with me. Same applies to the FBI. You're under instructions to talk to nobody. I'll contact New York CIA and they'll take over.'

'Do I answer questions?'

'Nothing other than routine. Jamieson's just a casual acquaintance. You know nothing about him. Terrible tragedy, can't understand why he should do it. The usual bullshit. Understood?'

'Yeah.' He paused. 'Did you do what we spoke about?'

'I don't know what you mean. We just had a cup of coffee as we waited for a car to take you to catch the New York plane. That's it. And anyway he's only a visiting Brit. We know very little about him.'

As he hung up there was a knock on the door. He opened it and the uniforms indicated one NYPD officer and one from Emergency Services. One of each.

The cop said. 'Can we come in?'

Goldman waved them in and closed the door behind them.

'What happened?' The cop looked around the room as he spoke.

'I've no idea. I was asleep and the noise of breaking glass woke me up. I looked for Jamieson and he wasn't around.' He shrugged. 'That's when I realised what had happened.'

The phone rang and Goldman lifted the receiver.

'Hello.'

'Frazier. Are the cops there yet?'

'Yes.'

'How many?'

'Enough.'

'Put him on. I'll talk to him.'

Goldman held the phone out to the NYPD man. 'He wants to talk to you.'

'Who is he?' the cop said as he took the phone.

'He'll tell you himself.'

'Rinaldi speaking. Who is that?'

'Officer Rinaldi, a senior CIA officer will be with you at the hotel any minute now. When he arrives he will take over and at that point he'll give you certain instructions. Meantime you will not discuss the incident with the officer who is there. D'you understand?'

'This is an obvious case of suicide in my precinct's jurisdiction. Who gave you permission to give any instructions to me as the NYPD officer in charge?'

'I've just been notified on my radio that the CIA officer concerned is on his way up to the hotel room. Just do as he tells you. Your senior NYPD officers have already been told what is happening.'

'I shall need instructions in writing before I hand over to any outside organisation.'

The phone was hung up at the other end and there was a loud knock on the bedroom door.

Goldman opened the door and a tall man walked into the room looking faintly aggressive.

'Right. Each of you give me your name and your reason for being here. Who's Rinaldi?'

Rinaldi said, 'Have you got some ID, mister?'

The tall man gave Rinaldi a dirty look as he lifted his mobile to his ear.

'Is Lieutenant Kowalski there?' He listened and then

said, 'Hi, Jan. I'm taking over now but I've got one of your bloodhounds here . . . name of Rinaldi . . . wants to play the smartarse. Would like everything in writing . . .' The man laughed as he listened. Then said, 'OK, I'll send him down to you. See you.'

He looked at the uniformed cop as he closed the flap on his mobile. 'Lieutenant Kowalski would be flattered if you joined him in the manager's office on the ground floor.'

The cop stared back and then headed for the door slamming it behind him as he left.

The tall man turned to Goldman. 'You don't need to know who I am but phone Frazier now and check it's OK.' He paused. 'While you're doing that I'll get them to move your kit to another room. I'll use this place as my base.'

As Goldman contacted Frazier he watched the hotel servants packing his two bags before handing him the keys for a suite at the far end of the corridor.

Frazier said, 'He's tall and loud. Likes throwing his weight about.'

'What about some positive ID?'

Frazier was silent for a moment. 'Get him to show you his left wrist. There's a small tattoo there, a tattoo of a scorpion. Give the bastard any help you can. He's on our side. Buries the bodies and tidies up the crap.'

The man pulled down the wrist of his shirt and said, 'You happy now? By the way, let's call me Tom, yes?' He paused. 'Who *was* the guy who jumped?'

'He was a colonel on loan to one of our special units.'

'Doing what?'

'Mathematics.'

'You mean he was a science doctor not a medic?'

'No he was a medic but a specialist in analysing test figures. It's called stochastic math. The mathematics of randomness.'

'What did he do for you guys?'

'He analysed the frequency of medical symptoms after the administration of certain drugs.'

'What kind of drugs?'

'Mind-control drugs.' He paused, hesitated, and then said, 'Mainly LSD.'

'What effect does that have?'

Goldman shrugged, hesitating. But Frazier had said tell the CIA man anything he wanted to know.

'We don't know. Different people react in different ways.'

'Is that the drug that Frazier used to lace the Brit's coffee?'

'Yes.'

'Why him?'

Goldman shrugged. 'He was there. Frazier's team are especially interested in reactions of people who don't know they've been given a drug.'

'So the Brit was there about this mathematical stuff and they drugged him without him knowing just to see how he reacted?'

'Yeah.'

'How *did* he react?'

'He became deeply depressed. He was supposed to catch a flight to London but he was in such a bad way when we got here to New York from Washington that Frazier wanted me to hang around with him to keep an eye on him.'

'Did he talk about suicide?'

'He was rambling about all sorts of things.'

'Including suicide?'

'Not in so many words.'

'Where was he posted from?'

'I'm not sure. I wasn't part of it. All I know was that he was a Brit, an officer on their General Staff and normally based at a military base in the UK.' He paused. 'By the way, what do I call you . . .'

'Like I said, just call me Tom.' He stood up. 'Did you see Frazier put the dope in the guy's coffee?'

'No.'

'So how do you know he did it?'

'Because he told me he'd done it.'

'Could have been joking. Pulling your leg.'

'We don't joke about LSD.'

'OK then. I've finished with you. If I need you again I'll contact Frazier.' He paused. 'If anybody else questions you, Police, FBI, State . . . whoever, you just know the guy was a bit down and then the noise woke you. That's all you know. Understood?'

'Yes. Understood.' He paused. 'What's going to happen now?'

The CIA man didn't respond and Goldman nodded to him as he headed for the door and his new room.

When he was alone the CIA man sat on the bed and started making a list.

1. Check morgue.
2. Take charge of anything on Jamieson's body and clothing.
3. Disconnect Jamieson from CIA to Pentagon.
4. Check names and addresses of Jamieson's family.
5. Check with Brit Liaison at Langley.
6. Check Jamieson's Brit unit.
7. Put someone to watch if insurance claim made on any US organisation.
8. Letter of condolence from Pentagon. No mention to Brit Liaison of Jamieson's time with CIA.
9. Get Goldman posted well away from Washington and NY. Small promotion.
10. Warning to HQ MK Ultra about Frazier. Too gung-ho for unsupervised activities.
11. When the dust has settled, study results of previous experiments on non-volunteers.

Chapter Ten

Swenson had suggested that they met at Georgetown University where they could eat and then find an annexe where they could talk.

In fact by the time they had finished their meal one of the staff had shown them to a small study and arranged to send in coffee for them.

When they had settled down at the small table, Swenson said, 'What's the problem, Joe?'

Maguire smiled. 'I feel I've been railroaded into a job that I know nothing about. Or very little.' He paused. 'You say I'm taking over from you but you're not a Senator, you're a retired general. Why couldn't I have had the same sort of arrangement?'

'Well, let me explain what I do and why my job has to be done by somebody more influential, politically influential that is, than a retired general.'

'It was part of our deal that I could be independent. Not a party stooge. Yes?'

'Yes.'

'So when I have to have views they're mine no matter whether they fit the Republican line or not?'

Swenson smiled. 'More or less, and we want you to be seen as independent.'

'So tell me what you do and what I'll be doing.'

'You'll be acting as sheep-dog for part of the CIA.' He paused. 'Do you remember me talking about an operation called MK Ultra?'

'Vaguely.'

'Put briefly, MK Ultra is concerned with mind-control. It uses drugs and it uses hypnosis for both intelligence gathering and for counter-espionage. MK Ultra is the most secret operation in the CIA.' He paused. 'And a lot of what it does is illegal or indefensible in any other context. It was given its authority from the highest level but it is not, repeat not, responsible to the man in the White House. If what MK Ultra does was made public, it would not only bring down the government but would leave us wide open and vulnerable to all those people and groups who want to destroy the constitution and the United States.' He paused. 'Are you shocked?'

'No. Surprised but not shocked. I've seen some pretty odd things in my work for the VA. But it seems strange that we have to accept that we need to protect the constitution by ignoring it ourselves.'

Swenson shrugged. 'It's one of those problems that the political philosophers argue about all the time.' He paused. 'If tolerance is a necessity of democracy, how much tolerance? Where do we draw the line? If democracy is giving power to the majority, what do we do when the majority can't tolerate the minority?' He smiled. 'You can read all the philosophy in any issue of *The New York Review of Books*. Both sides of the argument have been presented over the years and both remain unproven. MK Ultra has to deal with the realities of life in the real world, not in faculty discussions.' He sighed. 'And its barely worth recording that every Warsaw Pact country plus North Korea and China is using all the same methods against *us*.'

'I still don't understand what your role is or what mine will be.'

'Like I said, we need a sheep-dog or put in more human terms, we need a Father Confessor who watches what MK Ultra are up to and if he thinks it necessary he helps or hinders some particular activity.

'The problem up to now has been largely to provide a point of contact – me – whose views or whose word would be accepted by the Pentagon when very often it wasn't possible to present the real facts because they were too operationally secret or quite obviously in breach of the constitution. About a year ago we knew we needed some-body who could cover not only the military but the political angles. Somebody that all parties would trust.' He shrugged. 'That's when we decided that you were virtually the only candidate we knew who could cope with it.' He paused. 'You have to remember, Joe, that some of the rotten apples are in our own basket.'

'What about the people who voted for me? What do they get out of it?'

Swenson smiled. 'They'll be looked after, Joe. Knowledgeable people have done a draft plan of what needs to be done in the State and you'll have final approval on the main items.'

'When do you want me to start?'

'As soon as you can when you've wrapped up any obligations you have to the family law-firms and sorted out your finances. We are suggesting you have a consultancy role so that you get top-scale as if you were acting as a senior attorney. All expenses paid and how you set it up and go about it will be entirely up to you. But you'll have to be based here in Washington. Not in government facilities.'

'And I recruit my own staff?'

'Of course. It's all yours.'

'Give me a couple of weeks to sort out the basics and we can talk about the handover.' He paused. 'There's a mooring I want on the river and it needs approval by the City. Can you fix that for me?'

'I don't understand, Joe. Why do you want a mooring?'

'Because I'm going to live on a boat I'm buying. It'll be my home and in some ways my HQ.'

'Tell me about the boat.'

Maguire smiled. 'I didn't know you were into boats but it's a forty-five-footer. An Aqua-Star 45. Twin Volvo diesels. Fifteen-foot beam and beautifully fitted out. Three foot nine inches draught. Cruises at sixteen knots. Flat out twenty-three knots. Will cost me about four hundred thousand dollars including some personal modifications.'

For long moments Swenson was silent, then he looked across at Maguire and said, 'Joe Maguire, I've never heard you speak with such enthusiasm and affection about anything or anybody before.'

Maguire laughed. 'It's a kind of reward for a lifetime so far of doing what's expected of me. Some older guys go for beautiful bimbos to brighten up their days – and nights. Mine's just a very beautiful boat.'

'And this mooring business. I assume that the river you have in mind is the Potomac?'

'Yes. The mooring is part of a small boat repair, chandlery and gas station for boats. I can have mains electricity, mains water and they'll service it for me. I could have a telephone but I hope to get by with just my mobile. I need a permit to live on the boat and I thought that maybe your people could fix that.'

'If it's fixable. I'll fix it, Joe. Give me your mobile number. But remember you need to keep your official domicile as Wichita Falls or Austin.'

'That's no problem, they're both genuine residences.'

'And remember that only four people know that you have any connection with the CIA or the Pentagon.'

Chapter Eleven

———◆———

There were about twenty people at the funeral service at the Tunbridge Wells crematorium. Patrick King had said a few words about Richard Jamieson and they finished with a hymn: 'The day thou gavest Lord, is ended.'

The widow and the only child, a daughter in her early twenties, had gone back to the house in Goudhurst. The ashes would be available for collection the next day. Patrick King had made all the arrangements with the Americans about returning the body and they had been very helpful. They had advised him off the record that they had cremated the remains because it would be better for the family not to see the remains. They had borne the cost of the coffin and the shipment back to Tunbridge Wells.

Four people had gone back to the house in Goudhurst but only Patrick King had stayed after they had had tea and sponge cakes. Patrick King was thirty-four, a litigation lawyer and the fiancé of Jamieson's daughter, Emma.

There was sadness but no outward displays of emotion. The circumstances of his death were beyond their understanding and the Americans offered no theories on how it had happened or what caused it. The guilt from the suicide seemed to encompass everyone who knew the victim, like an ominous shadow. There was nothing to discuss. It was like something that happened in a night-mare that would be resolved in the light of day.

Patrick King had walked Emma Jamieson up the hill to the village churchyard and they sat on one of the worn, lichen-covered tombs, his arm around her shoulders.

'How is she taking it?'

'She's scared poor thing and it's going to alter things for all of us.' She shivered. 'For us as well, Patrick.'

'Why?'

'There are no savings, the Army won't pay any pension, they say it's the responsibility of the American Army. He was seconded to them and he died on active service.' She shrugged. 'Nobody's in any hurry and meantime we're broke with the bills piling up.' She sighed. 'I need to get a job that pays proper money and leave the legal training until we've got straight again. If we ever do.' He saw the tears at the edges of her eyes.

'Why don't we get married right now?'

'It's Mama. She'd never survive on her own. She'd just die of a broken heart.'

'She could live with us.'

'But she drives you crazy with her silly ways. Me too sometimes.'

'Sweetie, this is real life. She needs help. So do you. And I'd enjoy having you both with me.'

'You're just being kind-hearted. You'd regret it by the end of the first week.'

'I wouldn't, honey. I've given it a lot of thought before I suggested it to you.'

She looked at his face and said, 'I'm so lucky to have you.' And then her arms went round him and she rested her head on his shoulder.

Then she looked up at his face again. 'Let's go back and tell her, she'll be so — so pleased.'

'Let's get her organising our wedding. Where do you want it to be?'

'I'd kind of thought that if it happened we'd do it in the church but I think we'll do it nice and quietly at the register office.'

'We'll pretend that we're going to have a couple of days in Venice and spring it on her at the last minute that we're taking her too.'

She sighed as she shook her head. 'How am I ever going to repay you?'

'Have you spoken to a solicitor about the Army or the Americans paying both compensation and a widow's pension for your ma?'

'Thought of it but abandoned it. We haven't got the money to fight the government.'

'So appoint me to act for you and your mother. We might as well have a go.' He paused. 'Let me suggest it to her.'

Patrick King bought the Jamieson's house and the widow was able to carry on her old modest routine without having to worry about money. Emma had taken a fairly senior post with a group of local engineering companies and they had married quietly at the local register office and the only others present were Patrick King's parents. He had a successful law practice, and started the routine of applying for a pension by contacting the War Office and a local solicitor who was an old school-friend of his.

It took two months before he had been able to insist on a meeting with somebody responsible at the Ministry of Defence.

The man he saw was Leslie Ames. A man in his late forties who seemed not openly antagonistic.

'Are you saying that the widow of a serving officer who dies while on duty with the US Army is not entitled to a widow's pension?'

Ames pursed his lips and shrugged. 'Suicide of service personnel is always a problem area. When the officer concerned was on posting to another official body – in this case the US Army – it's even more complicated to establish where the obligation, if any, resides.'

'Can you give me details of the American army people who he was working with?'

'I'd have to consult my bosses before I could do that?'

'Why?'

'Protocol.'

'Would it help if I applied to a court here to be given what information I need to get the widow her pension?'

'I suggest that you could only do that as part of an ongoing legal action.'

'That's what I intend if I don't get satisfaction.'

Ames was silent for a few moments and then he said,

'I suggest you think very carefully before you go to law.'

'Why?'

Ames sighed. 'Because people don't commit suicide for no reason. You may not like what you hear if the thing is kicked around in court.'

Patrick King said quietly, 'That sounds very nearly a threat, Major Ames. If you know something relevant, I'm entitled to know what it is.'

'You realise that as Jamieson died in the USA, any court case would be heard there. Where he died. New York.'

'My case would be heard here and would not be about the circumstances of a suicide but the rights of an army officer's widow and her entitlement to a pension and maybe compensation for neglect.' He paused. 'One point I shall certainly be raising, Major Ames, is why we have had no details of an autopsy. And why the remains came to be cremated without any reference to Mrs Jamieson. I shall want the names and addresses of the people who made those decisions whether they are British or American.'

'I was told that the remains were in a terrible state and virtually unrecognisable. I think the Americans wanted to avoid upsetting Mrs Jamieson from seeing her husband's remains.'

'And the autopsy?'

'It was very much routine. There was no doubt about what the cause of death was.'

'What about the reason or reasons that made him take such a terrible step?'

'I think they brought in the standard statement for those circumstances. Killed himself while the state of his mind was disturbed.'

'Disturbed by what?'

Ames shrugged dismissively. 'Who knows?'

'Is there anything in his medical records that indicates any mental problems?'

'No. None at all.'

'Have you anything recovered from the body or his hotel room?'

'Not that I know of.'

'Could you check on that for me?'

'I'll see what I can do.'

Ames leaned back in his chair, his hands still on the desk-top.

'Why are you doing all this?'

'Major Jamieson's widow is my mother-in-law. There were no savings and no insurance but there ought to be a reasonable pension.'

Ames shrugged. 'I'll make some enquiries about his pension entitlement. But we're still left with the problem of who pays. Us or the Americans.'

King stood up, gathering his papers together and sliding them into his black leather briefcase.

'I'll write you a letter, Major Ames, on the points I've raised today. And your answers of course.'

Back in Tunbridge Wells King phoned a one-man research agency and gave them the date of Major Jamieson's death and asked for details of any newspaper reports, national or local, in the American press.

The following day he received fax-copies of two news items concerning Jamieson. One gave the name of the hotel where the death occurred and the other mentioned the name of the NYPD lieutenant who had acted as spokesman on the night concerned and subsequently at the precinct covering the incident.

A week later he got a letter from Ames in response to his letter outlining their consultation. The letter was a categorical denial that there was any obligation on the part of the Ministry of Defence to pay a pension to Jamieson's widow.

King booked himself onto a flight to New York in two days' time and he collected dollar travellers cheques and cash enough for a week in New York.

Lieut Jan Kowalski, NYPD based at Plaza One, was about the same age as Patrick King. A friendly self-confident man who was used to dealing with outsiders. An outsider being anyone who wasn't a member of the NYPD. He had not been involved in the hotel suicide business but had briefly read the files and remembered that way back when it happened his orders had been to say as little as possible, to refer persistent enquirers to the British Consul in New York or the Embassy in Washington DC. It was obvious from the summaries in the files that it was one of those CIA jobs that got swept under the nearest carpet. The US Embassy in London didn't want to be involved at any level but had pointed out to Washington that the enquirer, Patrick King, was the son-in-law of the deceased, was a very successful litigation attorney and had already been adopted as the Liberal Democrat candidate to stand for one of the Midlands constituencies at the next election. Worth assisting if appropriate.

King had booked in at the hotel where Jamieson had stayed. He had talked to the manager about the night of the suicide as if he was just vaguely interested and he had talked in more detail with the doorman who had been on duty that night and the maid who had been in charge of the room.

It seemed that the police had been on site within ten minutes of being notified but after twenty minutes or so some other authority had taken over and the police dismissed. The hotel records established that the bills had been paid by a company called Medical Resources (Arlington), and that whoever the people were who took over from the NYPD they gave no identification but the manager assumed that they were either FBI or CIA. He had received a call from somebody senior, a general or something, from the Pentagon. The call said that his staff should decline to answer any questions until a man named 'Tom' took over. After the takeover he should do whatever 'Tom' ordered him to do. He would not, repeat not, under any circumstances answer questions from the press, radio or TV. 'Tom' would deal with all that. The manager's description of 'Tom' was not flattering but indicated an aggressive personality with considerable authority, ready to treat even a moment's hesitation as deliberate obstruction. Jan Kowalski recognised a man typical of the kind of man he had to deal with frequently.

He had the file on his desk when King was shown into his office.

When the introductions and chat had been seen to, he said. 'What's your interest in this deceased, Mr King?'

'His widow is my mother-in-law and I'm trying to get your government or ours to pay her the widow's pension she is entitled to.'

'And being over here must mean that your own people are being negative?'

'So far, yes. But there seems to be some sort of agenda that I'm not being told about.'

Kowalski nodded. 'There's not much on the file. It was treated as a suicide but it looks as if it was taken out of our hands.'

'Was there an autopsy?'

'Yes. We carried out the autopsy but in these cases it's impossible to do a real job, the remains don't lend themselves to a thorough job. But it established that there was no alcohol in the blood.'

'There were no personal effects returned to his widow and that seems odd to me.'

'Could be a mistake. We could see if the morgue has anything. It could be just an oversight.'

'Who was it took over the case from the police and why?'

'I'm afraid I can't help you on that.'

'Can I ask why not?'

'It's restricted information.' He paused. 'You could ask the British Consul here in New York to see if he can help.'

'Will he know?'

'No.'

'Are you quite sure about that?'

'Quite sure.'

'That means it must be some security organisation like the CIA.'

'I'm afraid I can't comment.'

'Could you give me the address of the CIA office in New York?'

'Their address and telephone number are in the directory. It's public information.'

For a moment King thought of asking for the address of the morgue and then decided against it. He stood up.

'Thanks for your help.'

'I'm sorry I couldn't be of more help. But I have to stick to the rules.'

King asked the cab-driver to take him to the morgue without any idea of where it was or how it would be described in the telephone directory.

He joined a short queue at the enquiries window and ten minutes later he took his place at the window. He explained that he wanted to know if there had been any personal effects for the deceased.

He was referred to an office down a long corridor to a door marked 'Effects deceased'.

A woman clerk took the details of the deceased and the date of likely autopsy. King had waited for nearly an hour when the clerk came back with a small cardboard box.

'There's not much, Mr King. This is all we have. They must have forgotten to hand the stuff over to the coroner's office when they sent in the autopsy.' She sighed. 'But I'll have to have some formal proof that you can take over the box on behalf of the widow.'

King showed her his business card, a letter from Joanne Jamieson authorising him to act on her behalf in any matter, legal matters included. He also showed her his passport. Finally he was handed the package and he signed the form confirming that all the personal effects of the deceased – Jamieson L.R. – had been handed over to him as the legal representative of the widow, Joanne Mary Jamieson.

Back in his room at the hotel he opened the packet. There was just a leather wallet and inside he found a card stating that the holder, subject to offering the correct password, was entitled to entry into Areas A and MK in the establishment of Medical Research Resources Inc. There was a page torn from a small notepad with a note that said 'Speak to Frazier and Goldman before leaving'. On the reverse side of the page was a mathematical formula and in a flap in the wallet was an identity card in Jamieson's name and what looked like an elaborate mathematical formula with both numerals and letters. Below the long code was a signature and the letters MK Ultra (CIA). Also inside the flap was a small flat metal key. The kind of key that you get with a child's money-box.

As he laid out the various items on his bed, the phone rang. He wondered who could be phoning him. He hadn't told anyone where he was, not even the family.

He picked up the phone. 'Hello.'

'Is that Patrick King?'

'Yes.'

'This is Jan Kowalski. We met this morning.' He paused. 'I've just been informed that you picked up Jamieson's personal effects from the morgue after seeing me.' He paused again. 'This has led to a bit of a problem. It seems that the items were in safe-keeping in case there was any legal dispute about what was Jamieson's property and what belonged to the State.' Another pause. 'It seems that the staff at the morgue repository didn't have the authority to hand over the effects to you or anyone other than a court.'

'And?'

'And they ask that you return whatever there was to the morgue or, if it's easier, to me.'

'Unless someone is going to conduct some sort of enquiry, they're not entitled to Jamieson's property. It's the property of his widow and I've no intention of handing it over.'

There was a heavy, rather theatrical sigh from Kowalski and then he said, 'Can we talk off the record for the moment?'

'If you want to.'

'Can you tell me unofficially what was in the stuff they handed over to you?'

'It was just a rather worn leather wallet, small, pocket-sized.'

'Anything that matters inside it?'

'Yes. Various IDs and a few names.'

'Is there any chance I could have a quick look at them?'

'Oh. For heaven's sake, Jan. I'm a litigation lawyer and I don't offer my evidence to the other side if I can help it until we're in court.'

'I might be able to help you.'

'You're on the other side.'

'Let's meet and talk. You say you don't want to show

me what you've got but I'm not necessarily on the other side as you call it.' He paused. 'It could be off the record and just you and me. I've got an idea I could help you. Unofficially. You've got nothing to lose.'

'Why are you so interested?'

'The file on the incident is just one single page and it had too many loose ends. Instinct tells me that it was either a series of stupid admin cock-ups or it was a cover-up.'

'By whom?'

'By whoever took over from us, the NYPD.'

'So name names.'

'I'd be speculating but if I could see what you've got I could maybe be more precise.'

'And you'd tell me what you thought?'

'Yes.'

'No fudging?'

'No. Straight down the line.' He paused. 'I could be with you in twenty minutes.'

'OK. I'll wait for you.'

Back in his office Kowalski put down the phone and looked at the man who had been listening to him talking to King.

'If there's evidence there, what do I do?'

'Tell him enough to give him a lead but only to the CIA in general. No mention of this special operation.'

'Why are we doing this? Why help him at all?'

'Two reasons. The first to get it where it belongs, in Langley, not here with NYPD. And secondly, it might stop him pursuing it with somebody else.'

'Somebody else? Like who?'

'Like some politician hungry for a revelation, some-body in the media eager for a story . . .' he shrugged '. . . or anybody who doesn't like the CIA and the things it does that ain't in its brief.'

'OK. I'll phone you when I've got anything to report.'

'Phone me anyway. A nil report if it's appropriate.'

King noticed that Kowalski was dressed very casually. White sweater, chinos and Italian-style shoes. King was aware that Kowalski needed no persuasion to make him-self at home. But that was fair enough. This was his town. He and his colleagues made the rules. Ignoring the laws of the State or the country only when they could camouflage their actions as being essential in the pursuit of crime. It was Kowalski who got them started.

'The deceased guy, Jamieson, was your father-in-law, yes?'

'No. I only married his daughter after his death.'

Kowalski raised his eyebrows. 'So you've got a vested interest in the outcome of this affair?'

'Several vested interests.'

'I don't understand.'

'I've got a vested interest in seeing that the widow gets properly compensated. He was a serving officer and highly specialised. I've got a vested interest in finding out why an apparently perfectly normal man should commit suicide. A vested interest in knowing why the matter was taken out of the hands of the NYPD. And finally a vested interest in seeing that justice is done.'

Kowalski smiled wryly. 'Fair enough. What kind of guy was Jamieson?'

'He was about fifty. No medical problems apart from mild asthma. He was professor of mathematics at one of our regional universities. Published several scientific papers, and highly regarded.'

'D'you get on well with him?'

'I didn't see much of him but yes, he was an amiable man.'

'Hobbies?'

'Golf and photography.'

'Any money problems?'

'Just the usual ones we all have. No real problems.'

'Women?'

'Pro-feminism but didn't get worked up about it in public. Not a woman's man and I'd say was not terribly interested in sex. But not gay I hasten to add.'

'OK. Thanks for the rundown. How about we do a swap? I'll give you a photocopy of the NYPD report and you let me see the stuff from the wallet.'

'With one proviso, yes?'

'Tell me.'

'Whatever you find out from Jamieson's wallet you tell me.'

Kowalski shrugged and smiled. 'Fair enough.'

King pointed to the wallet and its contents on his bed, and Kowalski passed him a buff file with a single type-written sheet inside it. King read it and then put it aside waiting for Kowalski's comments. He took some time before he looked at King and said, 'What did you make of our report?'

'Somebody took over a police matter and warned the police not to record the details of why it was done, who did it and who authorised it.' He paused for Kowalski to comment but when he didn't King went on. 'I don't know enough about United States police procedures to suggest who was responsible but I'd guess it was the CIA.'

For long moments Kowalski said nothing and then he said, 'Yeah. It was CIA. On one of the CIA's special operations. That puts me in a spot. I've got a good general idea why they took over but if I told you, the least that would happen to me is that I'd lose my job. All I can do is to tell you to contact the CIA. They'll deny any knowledge of the incident. I'll give you the name of a lawyer who can help you.' He shrugged. 'I'm sorry but I can't do more. You'd better put Jamieson's stuff in a safe place. And be very careful who you talk to about it.'

'Tell me off the record what you think it's all about.'

Kowalski sighed and then said, 'I think it was some kind of drug-related experiment that went terribly wrong.' He paused. 'And I'd better warn you that they'll probably end up meeting what you want. But if you don't accept their final offer they'll play dirty rather than face being exposed by the media.'

Chapter Twelve

She was twenty-four years old and very pretty. Dark hair, big brown eyes and a trim body. He spoke gently and softly.

'How long have you been working here?'

'About six months.'

'Do you like the work?'

'Yes.'

'Now you've been promoted we'll be giving you even more responsibility. Does that worry you?'

'No.'

'You know that the work we do here concerns top-security files? And you would be responsible for the security of several hundred files?'

She smiled. 'That's no problem. I'm used to our security rules.'

'OK. Now look at this file and describe it to me.'

'It's like our standard security file. A brown cover, but this one has a red diagonal line about an inch wide from the top left-hand corner to the bottom right-hand corner.

It's a grade of file that is so top-secret that it can't be taken away from here by anybody.'

'What's the procedure for someone who wants to examine one of these files?'

'The applicant has to provide his ID and we take his fingerprints and the machine checks them against his prints on a card from an MK Ultra officer who has to confirm that the applicant can examine a specified file in one of our security closets where he will be locked in but in contact both ways by telephone. He will be rechecked every hour if he wants that much time. The guard will have given him a full search before he goes in the closet.' She shrugged. 'That's it.'

'Well done. Perfect.' He paused. 'I think you could start tomorrow. OK?'

She smiled. 'That's great.'

'See me tomorrow after you've finished.'

Six weeks later Fulton reckoned he could try her out. No drugs. Just hypnosis.

She sat there in the hard-back chair, her eyes closed.

'Tell me your name again.'

'My name is Joanna. Joanna Page.' Her words were slurred and she sighed after she had spoken.

'I want you to do something very special for me. Is that OK?'

'Yes,' she whispered. 'Whatever you want.'

'Look at the file I've given you.' He paused. 'Is it one of your top-secret files?'

'Yes.'

'How can you tell.'

'It's got the red line across it and you took it from the closet.'

'I want you to hide it inside your jacket and take it out of the building. When you get outside I want you to walk away to the right until you've counted up to a hundred. Then I want you to give the file to the first man you see and then walk away from him. If he speaks to you or follows you ignore him. If he persists, you tell him you'll call the police. Have you understood what I want you to do?'

'Yes.'

'Tell me what you have to do?'

She repeated the instructions he had given her.

'When I say "MK" to you I want you to wake up nice and slowly, stretch your arms and yawn. You won't remember what we've been talking about. Understood?'

'Yes.'

'It's for you, Joanna, it's MK for you. Wake up slowly . . . slowly . . . that's right.'

She stretched and yawned and smiled at him as he said, 'What were we talking about?'

She laughed. 'We were talking about Fred Astaire and Ginger Rogers.' He smiled. 'So we were. So we were. Well, we'll talk again tomorrow. I'll leave you to lock up. Take care. Be good.'

It was 10 p.m. when the call came through.

'Is that J. Fulton?'

'Who wants to know?'

'This is NYPD. Fifteenth Precinct. A guy handed in a file and a note in the file said to phone you if found. That's what I'm doing.'

'Thanks. I'll come down for it. Did the finder say where he got it?'

'Said a girl had shoved it into his hand and walked away. By the time he'd examined it she'd disappeared. He said she was early twenties and very pretty. Secretary type.'

'Thanks. I'll pick it up in about twenty minutes. Can I have your name?'

'Collins. Job 9581. Petty larceny section.'

Fulton put the girl into a hypnosis session twice a week until it became just a simple routine. She had stolen coded audio-cassettes from the radio monitoring section, phials of high-security drugs, keys and confidential reports. Although all the items were returned the thefts were real and unassisted. She had carried out Fulton's instructions meticulously but she had remembered nothing of what had happened when he released her from the hypnosis. When she was under hypnosis her name was Rosie. Her real name was Joanna Page. It was in the third month that Fulton risked testing his special theory. The theory of secondary hypnotism.

He had planned to carry out the second-stage experiment at the weekend and on the Thursday night he had gone over the file again. The file marked Operation Karla was a hotch-potch of typed pages, scribbled notes and a list of names, addresses and telephone numbers. He realised that there were few precautions he could take to cover things going wrong. The danger time would be getting her back to stage one again and then back to normal. Theoretically it must work but he was doing something that had never been done before. Maybe something that nobody had even thought of before.

Operation Karla was an attempt at hypnotising someone who was already hypnotised. Joanna Page would be put through the standard procedure, then hypnotised to her character of Rosie and then he would hypnotise Rosie to become Karla. Who, if his theory was right, could act in the second character, Karla, without Rosie knowing what had happened. A double security measure to ensure that Karla's life was totally secret. Joanna Page could be hypnotised by someone else but they would never know that Rosie was just a cover for Karla. It would be the ultimate deception. Control of someone who didn't even exist. A zombie.

Fulton had taken over the safe-house for the weekend. It was one of the old Georgetown houses. Old-fashioned but charming with geraniums and begonias in window-boxes and pale-blue shutters. The ground floor was living accommodation but the first floor was divided into five or six quite small rooms.

As if the whole of what he had planned wasn't risky enough, he had carried out the Rosie hypnosis at the office and then driven them both to the safe-house. As Joanna she would retain no knowledge of where the safe-house was located.

He had chatted to her as Rosie about the clothes she

was wearing and about the film they were going to see. A video of 'Zhivago'.

He tried not to hold his breath as he reached for her hand. She smiled and he said softly, 'Close your eyes and relax. Good . . . good . . . think of white snow.' He paused. 'Can you hear me?'

'Yes. White snow.'

'You're Karla. My best friend. Karla. Dear, lovely Karla.' He paused. 'Who are you?'

'I'm Karla.'

'There's a picture on the wall of a vase of flowers and a bowl of fruit. I'd like you to take it off its hook and put it on the table. When you hear me say "thank you, Karla", you'll do what I've asked. Yes?'

'Yes.'

Fulton had chatted to her for ten minutes or so and then he'd brought her back to being Rosie. She had yawned and stretched and stood up slowly, walking towards the window. Then he said, 'Thank you, Karla,' and she turned and walked slowly over to the picture, took it down and moved back to lay it on the table.

He had experimented for nearly two hours and it had been incredibly simple. It was crazy. It just worked. As if the theory was no more than an extra routine. There were bits and pieces of procedure to tidy up and then they had gone into the next room and watched the 'Zhivago' video. As he sat there with her he was conscious of his heart-beats. He had done it. All he had to do now was turn it into just another routine and on Monday they could decide how they would use her.

Chapter Thirteen

———————◆———————

Joe Maguire stood shading his eyes from the sun as the crane lowered the boat until it settled into the water. Two men released the canvas cradles that had held the boat. A boy was adjusting the plastic fenders on the starboard side.

In blue paint on the white transom it said, *'MV Aquila, St Peter Port, Guernsey, C.I.'* She had been built in Guernsey in the Channel Islands. It was the first of Aqua Star's new Ocean Star 45s to be shipped to the United States.

There was quite a crowd on the jetty to watch the arrival and there had been a ragged cheer as she settled in the water. One of the boat-builders' crew had tied the lines fore and aft. The engineer stayed for two hours and went over the Volvo Pentas and the electrical circuitry. The man was to spend the night in a spare bunk in the back of the chandlery and Joe Maguire was going to spend the night on the boat. He supervised the fuelling and filling the water tanks and, inevitably, when he was left alone in peace he turned the switches to warm up the diesels and then fired both engines. He was just about earth-bound enough to realise that he was listening to the noise made by roughly a hundred thousand dollars.

Swenson had offered to come over and help him celebrate the arrival but Joe Maguire wanted to be on his own. As the light began to go he checked that the mains cable was plugged in and then put on the riding lights and the lights in the cockpit, the saloon and the galley.

Being on the boat reminded him again of those wonderful weekends with his father on the thirty-foot cruiser on the Big Wichita river. They were almost the only memories he had of his boyhood. All that had ended when he enlisted, and a psychiatrist might surmise that the Ocean Star was a subconscious attempt to bring those days back again. Not that Joe Maguire himself had any such thoughts. For him it was another stage in his life. A treat he could well afford. But he would recognise that the pleasure wasn't just from the beauty of the boat itself, but in a kind of independence that living on a boat gave him. He could have bought the boat as a hobby but living on it was different. His father would have understood but Joe Maguire's colleagues saw it as some kind of aberration that came from growing older and a little eccentric. All the same, a few actually envied him. Not the boat but the irresponsibility. Maybe Swenson was the only one who recognised Joe Maguire's need for independence. Freedom from the stresses of Washington, the Pentagon and the CIA and the pressures to justify one more illegal operation. In the early days Joe Maguire had tried to establish in his mind where the borderline was between ruthlessness and illegality but he had soon given up the attempt. The situations were all different and there was no litmus paper for illegality.

He spent an hour reading the instruction book for the engines and looking at the circuit diagrams for the electrics. And finally he made up one of the single bunks, undressed and lay down, making himself comfortable, and read again a few pages of Hemingway's *For Whom the Bell Tolls* until he fell asleep.

Chapter Fourteen

———◆———

Kretski wasn't handsome but he was good-looking in an American sort of way and as he looked in the mirror over the basin he shaved very carefully. He didn't want to go through this thing with cuts all over his face. As he dried his face with a towel he looked at the girl on the bed and wondered if she really did love him. She was so beautiful he couldn't really believe his luck. But they'd been together for a year and it had been the happiest time of his life. She seemed happy too. But because of what he referred to as 'the circumstances' they had not lived a normal life. They couldn't be seen together in public. They might seem to a trained observer as too affectionate for her to be just his mistress. And even gossip could trickle back to Moscow and Ivana. That bitch would love to see him end up in the Lubyanka. He put on a blue shirt, a tweed jacket and light-coloured chinos. He kissed her as she slept and left a card on her pillow on which he'd scrawled the words 'Who loves ya baby'.

He had planned to use the pay-phone at the Choc Full

O' Nuts down the street by the bookshop. He had the scrap of paper in one hand and dialled the number with his free hand then put the receiver to his ear.

The man's voice was noncommittal. 'Washington bureau.'

'Is that CIA?'

'Yes.'

'I want to speak to a senior officer.'

'Hang on.'

There was a routine for dealing with that sort of request and the duty operator dialled the internal number of Grainger.

'I got one of those guys on the phone. Wants to talk to a senior officer.'

'OK. Put him through.' He heard the transfer click and said, 'My name's Grainger, how can I help you?'

'I'm a Soviet. I want to defect.'

'Where are you phoning from?'

'A pay-phone in a diner.'

'OK. But don't come here. D'you know Café Berlin on Massachusetts Avenue?'

'No. But I can find it.'

'I'll meet you there in half an hour. I'll get there before you and I'll be at a table with a coffee and reading today's *Washington Post*. OK?'

'OK.'

As Grainger hung-up, the internal phone buzzed. The phone service guy said, 'He was calling from a pay-phone at Choc Full O' Nuts.'

'Thanks.'

He slipped a mini-recorder into his jacket pocket.

Checked his ID and wallet and took a cab to Union Station and strolled back to Café Berlin, buying a copy of the *Post* on his way.

The café was busy especially around the delicatessen display and he made his way to a corner table and ordered coffee and an eclair. No need to be puritanical if you're about to interview a 'dangler', the CIA's name for voluntary defectors. They had roughly one a week. Half of them put-up jobs by the Russians and few of the others any use to the CIA. But you had to go through the routine in case you had the odd man out. A genuine defector. Not just a defector but a defector who'd got what you wanted.

He saw him as he came in and stood looking around, then he walked across slowly and Grainger said, 'I should have given you a password. Sit down. How about a coffee?'

'That's fine.'

When the coffee came Grainger said, 'What do I call you?'

'I thought maybe Tony.'

Grainger smiled. 'What's your real name?'

'Rudi. Rudi Kretski.'

'How can I help you?'

'I work at the Soviet Commercial Agency. I am political adviser. I want to become an American citizen.'

'Why?'

'It's a personal matter.'

'Not if you want to defect it isn't. We don't buy sight unseen.'

Kretski sighed. 'OK. I'm in love with a girl, an American girl. But I'm married in Russia. She hates me and I hate her.'

'These things happen, Rudi, but there must be other

ways to sort it out.' He paused. 'Tell me about your work at the Agency.'

'I comment on American reaction to things the Soviet Union is planning to do. And sometimes I comment on what I think is United States policy concerning the Warsaw Pact.'

Grainger smiled. 'How often are your forecasts right?'

Kretski laughed. 'More often than Moscow are.'

'What are they interested in at the moment?'

'They want to know American people's feelings about US embassy hostages held by the Iranians.'

'So what are our feelings about the hostages?'

'Real anger. I suggested that Moscow publicly make efforts to broker a deal of some sort.'

'Anything else?'

'They are very interested in Apple computer. They want to have software programs for the operating system.'

'Tell me something about the US that you think I don't already know.'

For long moments Kretski was silent and then he looked at Grainger. 'We are getting all the details of the US Navy's submarine control system. Navigation, target identification, communication systems, sonar camouflage, the lot.'

'How are they getting it?'

'From a US Navy man.' He paused. 'They've paid him over half a million dollars so far.'

'Do you know who he is?'

'He is not an officer. He just wants money.'

'Do you know his name?'

'No. It's not my area of operation.'

Grainger knew by instinct that Kretski was lying. He knew the game. And fair enough. You didn't put all you know on a plate at the start of negotiations.

'Let's get back to you. Tell me what you want.'

'I want citizenship and official recognition and protection. You find me a place to live and make it possible to marry my girl.'

Grainger shook his head slowly. 'Don't move from where you are living. Just carry on in your normal routine. I'll fix your passport and you don't need help to marry the girl. So long as she wants to marry you, just go ahead and do it, but as far as your job is concerned she's still just your girl-friend. Does she speak Russian?'

Kretski smiled. 'Just love words is all.'

As Grainger looked at Kretski it seemed crazy that a man who knew what Moscow's latest thinking was didn't know how to get himself a stolen passport. But that's how it was. Kretski needed a nanny.

'You're sure you want to go ahead with this?'

'Yes. Quite sure.'

'Let's just lay it out briefly. You'll tell us about what you're giving and getting from Moscow. And you'll take guidance from us about what you pass to them. And in return we'll fix your passport and documentation under any name and background you want. You'll be a consultant to us, the CIA, and you'll be paid by us for your work.' He paused. 'Is that a fair description?'

Kretski nodded. 'Yes. That's the deal.'

'D'you work office hours?'

'No. I'm free to do what I want.'

'I'm going to give you a phone number. You just tell

them you want to speak to me, Lew Grainger. They'll get me wherever I am. But always use a public phone. OK?'

'Yes. No problem.'

'I'll also write down an address where we can meet. It's a house in Georgetown. It's not an office.'

Grainger reached for the menu and tore off a strip and wrote down the phone number and the address.

As he handed it to Kretski he said, 'If whoever answers the phone asks who you are, you just say "MK". Understood?'

'When shall I phone you?'

'Every day, as near to six in the evening as you can.'

Lew Grainger had had meetings twice a week for a month with Kretski, and the Soviet section were enthusiastic about the operation. According to them Moscow's assessment of various areas of US policy were shrewder than they expected.

It was Grainger's idea that Kretski could be fed information that would distort Moscow's assessments but the problem was that Grainger was sure that doing that or even attempting to do that would unsettle Kretski. Distorting his comments to Moscow was bad enough, but deliberately sending back false information was too much. It was dangerous too. If Moscow even suspected that he was playing games their reactions would be immediate and ruthless. It was Charlie Brodsky who provided the solution. There was no need for Kretski to know that he was sending Moscow doctored information. He was a near-perfect subject for MK Ultra's speciality – mind control by hypnosis.

Lew Grainger had no medical qualifications but had learned by observation the routines for simple hypnosis. He was merely a fairly bright CIA man who had spent two years on the fringes of MK Ultra. There were several CIA men with similar backgrounds who, like Grainger, involved themselves in the medical conditions of people used by MK Ultra in their experiments. There were too many operations for time to be given to ethical supervision of what were themselves unethical experiments on unsuspecting human beings. But when Grainger went through the standard procedures of hypnotising Kretski it didn't work. Not even the simple basis of suggesting that he was tired and should close his eyes. He was sure that Kretski's resistance to being hypnotised was not deliberate. He was cooperative enough on everything else.

At the end of a month Grainger decided that he needed help from one of the drug specialists. Nothing outrageous, just something to relax the man and make him compliant. His contact was Lowther who listened to Grainger's story of his attempts at hypnotising the Russian. The drug that Dr Lowther gave him was the latest relaxant. Rohypnol. A drug that not only relaxed the recipient but left him with only a hazy impression of what had gone on even if hypnotism was not involved. When Grainger asked about side-effects, Lowther had shrugged. The drug was too new and still in the early development stage for any experience of side-effects. There had been some talk of loss of memory after three or four treatments but nothing serious. The memory recovered after a few hours.

Grainger waited for a weekend to try out the new drug and it worked completely. From inducing drowsiness, he went on to hypnosis and that worked too. When Grainger cleared Kretski from the hypnosis he seemed to remember nothing of what had gone on. He gave Kretski a carefully contrived item on US attitudes to current Israeli weapons development.

An ad hoc team had been assembled to work on the information to be passed on to Kretski. Some of it factual and some of it contrived to divert Moscow's interest from Israeli weapons programmes.

He had two normal sessions with Kretski before he gave him the treatment and fed him a complex description of a new encryption system that was being used by Special Forces units that was claimed to be unbreakable.

When the phone rang Grainger cursed and looked at his bedside clock. 2.15 a.m. He picked up the phone.

'Grainger. Who's that?'

'It's Kretski. Something's wrong.'

'Tell me.'

'I don't know where I am.'

'For Chrissake — ask someone.'

'They don't answer me. They back off. They think I'm drunk or on drugs.'

'Are you in a street box?'

'I think so.'

'What's the number on it?'

'I can't read it. Everything's blurred.'

'So how did you phone me?'

'A woman did it for me. I remembered the number.' He paused. 'There's a man here cursing me because he wants to use the phone.'

'Give him the phone. Ask him to speak to me.'

There was a jumble of voices, one of them loud and strident and the sound of metal clattering on metal. Then a voice said 'What the hell's goin' on? This guy's pissed out of his mind. Says you're his doctor or something.'

'Thanks very much for your help, sir. What did you say your name was?'

'Sears. Bertie Sears.'

'Mr Sears. My friend isn't drunk. He's ill. I don't know where he is phoning from. Could you perhaps help me and identify the call-box.'

'It's outside a bar called the Dial and I still think your friend's drunk. The bar is a few yards from the Metro stop.'

'Which stop is that?'

'It's on the red line. Woodley Park-Zoo.'

'Thanks for the information. Could I speak to my friend for a moment.'

'Sure. Here he is.'

'Hello.'

'Is that you Kretski?'

'Yeah.'

'Give the guy the phone and stay near the call-box. I'll be there in half an hour.'

Grainger was there in twenty minutes and as he paid off the cab he looked around. There was nobody using the telephone and very few people around. The bar was closed and there was no sign of Kretski. He walked around aimlessly for half an hour but knew it was pointless.

It was getting light when he signed in at Langley and checked Kretski's home address. It was in one of the small roads not far from the US Navy Observatory. He realised that he knew all too little about Kretski. He knew that he had no close friends either in his private life or his work at the Soviet Agency. He was preoccupied by the girl.

He waited to 8 a.m. before he pressed the bell. There was a radio playing that was switched off and footsteps came to the door. Kretski had shown him pictures of the girl but she was much more beautiful in reality. She was wearing a towelling bathrobe as she said, 'He's not here. Are you from his work?'

'Can I come in for a moment?'

She shrugged, hesitated, and then stood aside. She pointed to an armchair and said, 'Has something happened to him?'

'What makes you ask that?'

'He hasn't seemed well for some days. But he wouldn't let me call the doctor or the Agency. I think maybe he's been working too hard.'

'What was wrong with him?'

'He seemed confused. Agitated. Not knowing what was going on.'

'When were you going to be married?'

She looked surprised. 'Married? I was just his girl-friend. He talked about it but I wasn't interested. He would have been jealous of the other men.'

'What other men?'

She shook her head. 'Didn't he tell you? I'm a call-girl. He started off as a client and in the end I let him move in with me so long as he didn't interfere.' She paused. 'What's your interest in him?'

'Just a casual friend.'

He stood up. 'Will you ask him to contact me when he comes back?'

'Who shall I say?'

'Just tell him MK. He knows my number.'

For two weeks Grainger was on edge wondering if there would be a call from the police. He'd contacted the missing persons bureau but there was nothing. Instinct told him not to mention the missing Russian to anyone at MK Ultra.

Over the next four months he had contacted the girl several times but she had no news of Kretski and was obviously not much concerned about the missing man.

It was overhearing a casual conversation between two CIA men in the canteen that had reminded him of the missing Kretski. The CIA man who was in charge of keeping an eye on all Soviet official organisations in Washington had said casually, 'The Commercial Agency are getting a lot of stick from Moscow. Seems they've been covering up one of their guys who's done a runner. Just disappeared.' He laughed. 'They even had the brass neck to ask the police to help find him, and the police asked if the guy was officially now a refugee.'

Grainger left without drinking his coffee and wondered what the reaction would be if sometime Kretski turned up and told them what had happened. According to the doctor who gave him the Rohypnol, the effects should have lasted no longer than ten days at the maximum. He was uneasy about it for the rest of the day but by the following day he had put it out of his mind. Just once during that month he'd entertained the foolish thought of visiting Kretski's girl-friend as a client rather than as Kretski's friend. But the thought of the complications that could cause were enough to make him ignore the crazy impulse.

Chapter Fifteen

———◆———

King had been in New York for just over two weeks and when his phone rang in his room at the hotel he didn't recognise the voice at the other end.

'I'm sorry I didn't catch your name.'

'It's Ames. Major Ames, we met in London some time ago about the Jamieson case. Remember?'

'Yes. Of course. How did you know where I was?'

'I phoned your house and your wife gave me your number.' He paused. 'How're you getting on over there?'

'I'm getting there. Slowly.'

'I think I could help you. If I came over could we meet and talk?'

'How can you help me now when you couldn't help me before?'

'I've been making a few enquiries.'

'So let's talk right now.'

'I think you already know that this sort of thing can't be discussed on the phone.'

'Why not?'

'It's a question of security.'

'Are you sure it's worth the journey for you?'

'I'd be surprised if you didn't find what I had to say would save you a lot of time and trouble.' He paused. 'And make a satisfactory solution to the problem.'

For a few moments King was silent and then he said, 'When did you intend coming over?'

'I could be with you tomorrow. I'll stay at the Waldorf.'

King sighed. 'OK. I'll expect to hear from you when you're ready to talk.'

It had been mid-evening when Ames phoned. He had already eaten and could come across straightaway.

When King opened the door to Ames he was surprised for a moment that he wasn't in uniform. And then realised that you don't wear uniforms in a foreign country. He looked more like a senior IBM executive in his well-cut, dark-blue suit and a black leather briefcase under his arm.

They went through the rather stilted social chat bit and settled down in facing armchairs.

Ames said, 'What sort of progress have you made?'

King shrugged. 'I checked on the address of the company who picked up both hotel bills. One for Jamieson and the other for a guy named Goldman. The address was a used-car lot and the rest of the buildings were mainly rubble. The so-called Medical Resources (Arlington) is just a paper company.

'I tried a commercial research guy to check on what was filed on the company. He used a lawyer's outfit to do it and they came back and said that it was a CIA cover for moving small sums of money around. That fitted in with some things I had found when I got Jamieson's belongings from the morgue.

'I made friends with a Lieutenant Kowalski of NYPD. He was very cagey but when he saw a piece of paper from Jamieson's stuff that had the names Goldman and Frazier and another piece of paper that just said MK Ultra, Kowalski was obviously very agitated.

'I've tried a retired FBI man to check on the two names. He obviously knew something about what MK Ultra is and backed off. But he confirmed that both names were of men who worked for the CIA but didn't appear in their official records. He said I could assume that I wouldn't get any further.'

'Do you think you can get further?'

'Yes. I'm sure I can. It's a good story for any newspaper. Public sympathy will be on the side of my client even if he is a Brit.'

'It'll make a good story but it'll finish off any chance you've got of getting a pension for the widow. The CIA play by the big boys' rules.' He leaned forward. 'What amount of money are you looking for?'

'I checked at the War Office press unit and they gave me fifteen to seventeen thousand a year as he was a specialist.'

'They could use the suicide to say it was self-inflicted and therefore make a reduction.'

'A suicide almost certainly due to stress caused by his work for your people.'

'How would you prove that?'

'He has no record of depression or stress before he was

seconded over here. I'd have to take it to court.' He paused.
'I don't know what it's all about but I've got a strong feeling
that your people are desperate to hide something.' He
paused again. 'I think you know that too. That's why
you're here.'

'Can I ask you a fundamental question?'

'Go ahead.'

'If I had been able to agree to a full pension for Mrs
Jamieson, would that have settled the matter?'

'It would have then but there's more involved now.'

'Like what?'

'Like the Americans. Like whatever this MK thing is.'

'But your main concern, even now, is to get a fair deal
for Mrs Jamieson.'

'It won't be easy to get a fair deal from two governments
who are so mean-minded that they deny responsibility for
paying a normal service pension to a senior officer. An
officer who died in the course of duty.'

'What if both governments accepted responsibility and
Jamieson got full pensions from both parties?' He frowned.
'As I work it out that would give the widow a life pension
of just over forty thousand a year.'

'Dollars or pounds?'

'Pounds sterling.'

'I'd need to talk to Mrs Jamieson.'

'Would you recommend her to accept?'

'If she opted to take it I'd go with it.' He paused. 'In
fact I'd be prepared to recommend acceptance. With one
proviso.'

'What's that?'

'That some senior CIA man told me in confidence what had actually happened.'

'Would a US Senator be senior enough?' He paused. 'He's not CIA but he has a watching brief covering them.' He paused again. 'I'd go so far as to let you talk to him before you contact Mrs Jamieson.'

For the first time King felt that the other side were trying to play fair. Or somewhere near it.

'OK. I'll go with that.'

Joe Maguire was old enough to be Patrick King's father and despite the fact that King had never been a soldier and was in an adversarial position they had taken an instant liking to each other.

They met at King's hotel in New York and Joe Maguire wasted no time.

'Is it OK to call you Patrick?'

King smiled. 'Of course, sir.'

'Yeah. And I'm Joe.' He paused. 'And right now I'm not a Senator nor an Army officer and no wiser than the next man. I'm Joe. And I'm hoping to put something right that went horribly wrong when your father-in-law died. You're a lawyer and I was a lawyer for some years.' He smiled. 'Long years for me. I wasn't born to be a lawyer. Too impatient. Too eager to find a solution that would satisfy both sides.'

Patrick King smiled. 'I asked around and everybody said you could have made a fortune if you had stuck to the law and ignored the problem of justice.'

'You know it's strange but making a fortune has never interested me all that much.'

King smiled. 'Even lawyers have to eat.'

Maguire smiled. 'People tell me my taste in food belongs in a sergeants' mess-hall.' He paused. 'But there's a serious point in all this and that's what do you do with your fortune. If there's one thing I've learned kicking around it's that money's not really much use. In fact, so far as I'm concerned it's only got one use. Beyond a place to live and all that domestic stuff, money has only one use. And that's to be able to tell the rest of the world to get lost. Independence for me is everything.' He smiled. 'I mustn't indulge in sermons and I mustn't waste your time.' His face was serious again.

'What I've got to tell you is a sad story. Colonel Jamieson was the victim of a piece of thoughtless stupidity. The people he worked with here were specialists in using drugs for mind-control. He was no part of it himself. From time to time drugs were given to people who didn't know what was happening. It was a kind of test to see what effect a drug had on someone who didn't know it was being administered. The man who administered LSD to Colonel Jamieson was a highly qualified medical guy and to put it bluntly a monstrous asshole. He still can't believe what happened from his stupid act of lacing Jamieson's coffee with a minute drop of LSD.

'I can assure you that it was a foolish accident. No harm was intended. As you know there were frantic efforts to sweep it all under the carpet. It succeeded until you came on the scene and both sides, the CIA and your Ministry of Defence, behaved like the worst type of shysters. Between us you and my lot have come to an agreement provided none of it is made public and that you believe my good faith.'

Patrick King didn't hesitate. 'I'll accept what you've told me, Senator, and I'll sign the papers on the compensation for Mrs Jamieson.' He paused. 'Thank you for trusting me.'

'If you're ever in Washington I'll show you my boat. I live on a boat.'

King smiled. 'I heard about the boat. It sounded a great idea so long as there's no family planned.'

They agreed to keep in touch but they both accepted that this meeting was the end of the sad story.

Chapter Sixteen

He was on the telephone at his desk as she walked into his office and he waved her over and pointed to the comfortable seat facing him.

She watched him as he listened. Senator Joe Maguire was in his late sixties. Handsome, with a big Roman emperor's face and broad-shouldered with a big frame. She had known him for most of her life. From the days when as a five-year-old she'd been taken by her father to see Joe doing his stuff for the college football team. She guessed there must be a least fifteen years between them. He had graduated, but not spectacularly, and some said he'd only scraped through because of his football prowess.

She had lost touch with him for several years and it was only when she saw him at his sister's graduation that she had heard that he was in the army and doing well. After that it was just odd rumours that he had been a lieutenant-colonel when he left the army, and he had been recruited into the CIA before he joined his father's law firm in Wichita Falls.

She had seen a lot more of him when he moved into politics and she was working for the Democrats. Joe Maguire was a natural-born Republican with most of their vices but with a genuine, friendly charm that served both him and his party well. He had a reputation for loyalty and even-handedness. But he wasn't going to like what she had come to tell him.

As he hung up the phone with one hand, he reached across with the other to cover her hand as it lay on the file in front of her.

'Annie. It's great to see you. How're you making out these days?'

She smiled. 'I'm getting by, Joe.'

'I heard they're putting you up for the Supreme Court.' He grinned. 'The Democrats love their token women.'

'Well this token woman is here officially so I'd better get on with it.'

He smiled and shrugged. 'It's all yours.'

She sighed and then said, 'Tell me about MK Ultra.'

He looked shocked and for long moments he was silent, then he said very quietly. 'How about you tell me?'

'Let's not play games, Joe. You're in a mess.'

'What kind of a mess?'

'Every kind you can think of. Illegal use of Federal funds, drug abuse, abuse of military and civilian personnel.' She paused. 'D'you really want more, Joe?' She shrugged. 'There's plenty more if you want it.'

'And who's gathering up this kind of crap?'

'The Secretary of State who's fending off a very irate British Ambassador. The Armed Services Committee, the Joint Intelligence Committee, the Justice Department, the Pentagon, you name it and I can fit 'em in somewhere.'

'What did you say this thing was called?'

'Don't bullshit me, Joe. You know damn well what it's called. MK Ultra, brainchild of the CIA who swear it doesn't exist and never existed.' She paused and watched his face as she said, 'I've heard the word impeachment floating around. Take it from me it's very, very serious.'

'And what's your part in all this?'

'To ask you what goes on.'

'And then?'

'We want to avoid having them take action against you.'

'Why?'

'Because I can't believe that a man like you would get involved in things like this without good reason.' She paused. 'I can't imagine what good reason that could be but I want to hear your reasons from you.'

'How far has this gone?'

'All the way. Right up to the top man. He had to be told because of the possibility of impeachment.'

'Why are they using you?'

'Because they know that I know you from way back and will understand you better than a politician could. And because I'm a judge and bound by oath to protect the constitution.'

'How long have we got? To talk I mean.'

'A month at the outside.'

For long moments he was silent and then he looked at

her face. 'Doesn't a democracy have a right to defend itself? Do we always have to sit there and take it from people whose only wish is to destroy us?'

'You'd better tell *me*, Joe.'

'It goes back a long way. How much time can you give me?'

'All day, every day.'

'Do I need a lawyer?'

'I don't know but you can't have advice. This is under the same rules as going in front of a grand jury. No lawyers, no witnesses.'

He stood up slowly. 'How about I take you to dinner?'

'No thanks. Let's say 8 a.m. here tomorrow morning.'

He shrugged. 'OK.'

He walked with her to the door, opening it slowly as if he were loath to let her go.

The doorman saluted her as he swung back the main door of the apartment block for her. She smiled and nodded as she walked over to the desk for her post. Most of her mail went directly to her office and she kept her home address out of the reference books. As she went up in the elevator she remembered that her mother was looking forward to seeing yet another TV re-run of *The Godfather*. Her mother was convinced that if only she had been there to have a word with all those silly men all would have been well. She had once pointed out to her mother that if it had all been well there would have been no film, which comment had only confused her mother.

She'd got a pizza for the two of them and they could eat as they watched the TV. Her mother had had a good day. She suffered from arthritis, and she sat in the kitchen as Judge Annie Cooper prepared their meal.

'You were late tonight. I thought we weren't going to make the film.'

'Yeah. I had an extra meeting.'

'Anybody interesting?'

'D'you remember Joey Maguire?'

'You mean Moira's boy? The pudgy one.'

'That's the one. He's not pudgy now. He's a Senator and Senators are well-built not pudgy.'

'How'd he get to be a Senator? I thought he was in the army in Vietnam.'

'So he was Momma. But that's a long time ago.'

'I can't keep up with these things you know.' She sighed. 'Senator, uh. How'd he do it?'

She bit back her inclination to say 'by licking a lot of arses' and said 'Working hard, Momma. And making friends.'

'Is he married?'

'He was but I think they were divorced about ten years ago. She was old man Miller's daughter. The very pretty one, Carole.'

'Was he good to her?'

'Who knows. They looked like they were happy. But who can tell.' She paused. 'Now you get ready in your TV chair and I'll bring this stuff in on the trolley.'

As she watched the credits come up for the film her mind went to Joe Maguire. She smiled to herself as she recalled her mother's comments and questions. Her father used to say he could tell what a man was like from his shoes. Her mother, eternally feminine, wanted to know if he was good to his wife. Maybe there was a thin streak of logic in there somewhere. But you could wipe out most of Congress if that was the criterion. She was a judge and at the same time she was part of the political establishment, but she was no admirer of politicians. And if her analysis of Joe Maguire was correct he too was not impressed by the political circus and its performers. He was usually described as 'a man's man', whatever that might mean. It had a vague ring of truth about it because he had been good at all those manly things from semi-pro football through soldiering and the CIA to a landslide victory as Senator for his home State with never even the faintest suggestion of dishonesty or self-seeking. His background was moneyed enough and his nature was friendly and concerned. She wondered what kind of people and what kind of arguments they had used to turn this all-American boy into the monster in that thick file in her briefcase.

She sighed. She wasn't going to enjoy the next few weeks. She was well aware that she had been sent on a fishing expedition. The special committee's 'evidence' was based on anecdote and gossip with a few facts thrown in as make-weight. And there was no statute or amendment that would warrant them offering what she was doing to a grand jury. The ad hoc committee might have right on its side but they knew all too well that any politician who chose to reveal what was going on inside MK Ultra could count his career as over. There were at least two of them who were genuinely glad that they were trying to bring to an end an operation that was one of the CIA's weapons against Communism. They knew so little but they knew that they knew enough. Or maybe too much.

Tape 1

It was an implied part of the deal that I worked out with Annie Cooper (then, Judge Anne Cooper, and now, Associate Justice of the Supreme Court of the United States), that I'd tell her what MK Ultra was all about. Since thinking about it I realise that there's nobody on this earth who could do that. I was its 'guardian angel' for many long years but the operation was so secret and so diverse that nobody, including me, could be sure where it began or ended. So I'm going to tape what I can remember, but it won't be chronological. Just bits and pieces as I remember them. I shall change a few names and place-names but the rest is, for better or worse, actual fact.

My name's Joseph Maguire and I'm Senior Senator for the State of Texas and have been so for many years. By the way, the Maguire bit is Scottish not Irish. My old mother, bless her soul, always told girls I brought home that they ought to know that I was a Scorpio, and Scorpios, she warned, were trouble-makers.

Tape 2

I don't think that anyone knows what the real start-date was of the MK Ultra operation. It went at least as far back as 1947 but in those days its codeword was Artichoke. The whole concept came out of what we thought the Koreans and the Chinese were doing to control people's minds by using hypnotism and drugs. MK Ultra wasn't just a United States thing, there was a lot of highly respected institutions and organisations in the UK who contributed large sums for its funding and leading staff on the medical side. As Artichoke began to accumulate some successes and failures, it grew very quickly and it was in April 1953 that Allen Dulles authorised the MK Ultra programme in his role of CIA Director. His authorisation laid out simply and clearly the guidelines.

This is a brief extract of that authorisation that shows that nobody was kidding anybody, right from the start.

'Precautions must be taken not only to protect operations from exposure to enemy forces, but also to conceal these activities from the American public in general. The knowledge that the agency is engaging in unethical and illicit activities would have serious repercussions in political and diplomatic circles.'

I knew all too well that describing exposure of MK Ultra as having 'serious repercussions in political and diplomatic circles' was a euphemism that was like describing the San Francisco earthquake as a building problem.

And whatever you could say about Allen Dulles he was neither a crook nor a psychopath. For me Dulles was a patriot. Maybe patriotism can go too far or give cover to less honourable attitudes. Who knows? And who's to judge? Not politicians for me. Like Harry Truman had said – 'If you can't stand the heat, get out of the kitchen.'

Tape 3

Looking back at the early days of MK Ultra I realise now that it was inevitably going to end up out of control. The CIA wanted to control minds but didn't know how to do it. The doctors, the psychiatrists, the neurologists claimed that they could do it and the CIA could take over the results.

If there was one point, one decision that spelled eventual disaster for MK Ultra it was made at the meeting when the specialists claimed that experimenting with drugs on volunteers was useless for CIA purposes. They needed to be able to experiment on people who didn't know that they were being used. Volunteers would give a false picture of the effects of drugs and could distort the effects of hypnosis. It was up to the CIA people to give the go-ahead or close down the operation. The chance of having such control over people's minds was too good to abandon and the decision was made. The medics could use non-volunteers.

I wasn't around MK Ultra at that stage and if there were abuses they weren't apparent. The experimenters were men loaded with qualifications and highly respected at universities, medical schools and in scientific circles. But I realised early on that the kind of men who wanted to control people's minds would be ruthless in the pursuit of their experiments.

Maybe it's worth mentioning that thirty years after I first met Col. Swenson it was Lieut. General (Retd.) Swenson who handled my campaign for being elected Senator for Texas. And I'd better confess that despite the promotions in the army and later in the CIA, being Senator for Texas is the only achievement that I'm really proud of.

Tape 4

It was almost a year after the election that I was able to piece together what Swenson had been up to and the strings that had been pulled by the CIA and a number of Republican politicians including members of Congress.

To them it was just one of the many 'arrangements' they made when they cashed in old favours in what they considered was a good cause.

Apparently the only snag was of my doing when I said categorically that I wouldn't stand as a Republican, only as an Independent. Some of them saw it as an affront to the Party but others thought it was a winning move.

For me the campaign was like being caught up in one of those twisters that destroy everything in their paths. But to tell the truth I was flattered that men of such power and experience saw me as a potential Senator. It was something that had never entered my mind but they had caught me at the right time. For two years I had been aware that I was bored. The first year of setting up the new office had kept me busy with organisation and looking for new clients, but by the end of that first year our new office was as stable and solid as our main office. It seemed incredible but I realised that I missed my life in the army.

Although I wasn't aware of it at the time, the army was my home.

I belonged in the army from the day I joined and if you like the army it recognises it and rewards you accordingly. The old China hands always said, 'Don't volunteer for anything', but I'd gone the other way and volunteered for everything that was on offer. Parachuting, advanced map reading, unarmed combat, survival courses and eventually a long stint in Special Forces. When those days were over I had been made a Staff Officer and it was then that I specialised as a trouble-shooter. Smoothing ruffled feathers and pouring oil on troubled waters. Frequently ignoring service protocol to turn bitter rivalries into reasonable working relationships with both parties satisfied that they'd had a fair deal. I'd left the service at the usual retirement age without any great thought about what I'd do.

The law degree and joining my father's firm seemed the obvious route to go. But looking back I realise that the change from constant action and decision to the steady routine of civilian life was unsatisfying and very near to being boring.

That six months had given me a fair picture of what things could be like if I made it to Austin in November. But the last two months had shown me how the media tried to control and influence the public. The TV news people were the worst. They had more money behind them than radio or the newspapers and magazines. Early on in the campaign I was told that one of the big networks was building up a 'devastating' story about my private life to be broadcast nearer election date. It turned out that the great revelation was to feature my divorce. But both Carole and her parents told the bastards that they were not only still good friends of mine but would vote for me on the day.

It had taken nearly five years for Carole and me to realise that we were more like brother and sister than lovers or husband and wife. Neither of us had anything to complain about concerning the other. We just didn't belong. The divorce itself was without rancour and I don't think either of us suffered in the process. I remembered hearing someone say that I had only married Carole because she was so like my mother. Bearing in mind that I didn't really care for my mother, nor she for me, it seemed a strange misjudgment. I wasn't given to philosophising or analysing motives and characteristics in those days and if I had been pressed to do so I wouldn't have said that it was anything more than proving that marrying the girl next-door doesn't always work out. We have kept in touch over the years and I'd heard that she is now happily married with two children. Her husband was some kind of artist.

A couple of weeks after the inauguration, Swenson had told me that they wanted me to take over his job. 'They' were apparently the CIA, some top people at the Pentagon and several members of the Senate Intelligence Committee.

Chapter Seventeen

She wondered if he might keep her waiting just to make a point. But he didn't. He was already there, waiting for her.

They exchanged the traditional pleasantries as she riffled through the papers in her file. When she found what she was looking for she leaned back in her chair and smiled at him.

'You won't be surprised if I tell you that the Pentagon and the CIA both swear that they have no record of your having served with their organisations.'

He shrugged. 'What is it you want to know?'

'Your family doesn't have a military background and you must have been very young when you joined the army.' She paused. 'Why *did* you join?'

He smiled and shrugged. 'It was a good excuse for leaving college.' He paused. 'And I needed to get away from my dull background.'

'But they gave you your degree.'

'That was just a gesture to the football coach.'

'And the CIA?'

He shrugged. 'For now I plead the Fifth but we can talk about it later if you really want to.'

'Joe, it's your connection with the CIA that makes you vulnerable so why not let's get it over with?'

He sighed. 'Because you wouldn't understand.'

'Why not?'

'Because you're too young. You had to have been through those times to understand.'

'So tell me about those times.'

'I guess you might just about remember the background to Vietnam. The slaughter, the body-bags, the insults to our veterans by our own people.' He shifted in his chair as if the thoughts made him uncomfortable. 'Vietnam was the second time around. We'd done it all before in Korea.' He paused. 'Tell me what you know about the Korean war.'

'MacArthur, the Chinese and the Russians. The forty-ninth parallel.'

He laughed softly. 'Forty-ninth parallel was a film about the US-Canadian border. It was the thirty-eighth parallel in Korea.'

'Were you in Korea?'

'Yeah. Two years, nearly three. It taught me a lot.'

'About what?'

'About politicians and the facts of life.'

She frowned. 'Facts of life? Surely you heard about those back home.'

'Not the facts of real life.'

'Like what?'

'That a man's arm or his leg is very heavy to pick up when it's not attached to a body and that if you pick up a head by the hair the skin'll come off. Those facts of life.

And what to do if you end up collecting too many left feet to match the right ones.'

For long moments she was silent and then she took a deep breath and said, 'How old were you then?'

He shrugged. 'Eighteen, nineteen, twenty. Thereabouts.'

'A bit early to be disillusioned about politicians.'

'It was politicians who restricted what MacArthur could or couldn't do and politicians who sent our troops to face the toughest army in South-east Asia. We were outnumbered ten to one, their highly-trained fighting troops against our novices. They had weapons and artillery and tanks that were far superior to what we had available. And when the chips were on the table the politicians laid down that MacArthur couldn't cross the Yalu or fly over the Chinese border. They were kicking the shit out of our boys and we weren't allowed to kick back.' He paused. 'We lost nearly as many lives in Korea as we did in Vietnam. And still the commies challenge us thirty years later.' He paused again. 'And any way we can beat them is legitimate as far as I'm concerned.'

'Any way?'

'Yes. No holds barred.' He paused and looked at her. 'And I'll say it in public too if you and your friends want it that way.'

'It's an enquiry, Joe, at the moment, not a prosecution.'

'Your Democratic friends won't relish having to align themselves with the commies. And that's what they'll have to do.'

'You sound like Senator McCarthy, Joe.'

'McCarthy wouldn't have recognised a commie if he

saw one. His was a political ploy. My views are based on experience.'

'I saw a cutting that said you were a colonel when you left the army. You were very young for that rank. You must have liked the army.'

'I liked the people and I got things done.' He paused. 'Who are you after – me or the CIA?'

She shrugged. 'You know all too well what it's like with these sorts of committees. Lots of axes being ground. Old rivalries given another run. Old scores being settled and one thing traded for another – like votes in the House.'

'Who's aiming at me?'

'Not so much you. It's just that you're a link in the chain. A lot of links in fact. Your name keeps popping up around the edges. And . . .' she smiled, '. . . you're a hero, much respected and beyond reproach. That in itself is enough for some people to have a go.'

'How much do the media know?'

'Nothing from the committee but there have been hints in the press over the last couple of years that I've got in the cuttings. Nothing recent.'

'And what's the objective of the committee?'

'To put a stop to the kind of capers that MK Ultra has been getting up to.'

'Nothing more? No heads rolling?'

She smiled. 'Joe, dear. You need evidence for anything more. And *that* we ain't got.'

'So if the operation is closed down that's the end of the story?'

'So far as my lot are concerned – yes.'

'How long can you give me?'

'How long do you need?'

He closed his eyes, thinking, and then he said, 'It's a very complex set-up, Annie. I'll need at least six months to a year to unscramble it. If I can't then meet what you want I'll tell you – but nobody else.'

'She nodded. 'OK, Joe. It's a deal.'

The committee were eventually more or less satisfied with what she had arranged. They had no hard evidence and no witnesses, certainly no witnesses who would be willing to testify to a grand jury. They had long experience of jousting with the CIA and the agency had always prevailed. Even the agency's angry denials of the existence of MK Ultra was something of a victory.

Senator Maguire had recognised that MK Ultra was under real pressure but there was a vast administrative network to untangle. Hundreds of highly-qualified people to dispose of, the problems of subjects under treatment and the loss of key figures in the programme and the help that they were giving to the CIA. He decided that he would keep two much-reduced MK Ultra teams and consider moving at least one of them from the United States. The rest would have to go. Fortunately many of them were part-time and all of them were highly qualified and would be welcome at many institutions and universities. Meanwhile he had to decide on no more than a dozen who would be the nucleus of the two units still continuing their work and decide what existing operations would be continued.

Chapter Eighteen

He loved the white convertible MG but he knew he'd have to change to something with air-conditioning. Florida, even alongside the Gulf of Mexico, was already too hot at 8.30 a.m. to be tolerable. He missed Vermont and the woods. He tried to remember the words of the Shakespeare sonnet: *'Full many a glorious morning have I seen — something, something — kissing with golden face the meadows green, gilding pale streams with heavenly alchemy'*. And then the automatic arm on the gate swung upwards and he drove past the notice that said simply — US Army — Keep Out. He sighed. There were neither green fields nor an echo of Shakespeare in the sixty acres of arid land that was the site of what was logged as Army Medical Supply Depot 77.

Following the dusty drive he passed the sprawling buildings that housed the stores and laboratories and pulled in behind the breeze-block building that stood apart from the rest. There was no need to lock the car and he used his swipe card to open the door marked MK and walked down the corridor to his office. The notice on the door said, 'Col. H. Rogers'. He put the fingers of his right hand on the sensor and waited for almost a minute while the database sorted out his fingerprints before the door slid open with a gush of cool air from inside.

Inside, the walls and ceiling were painted white. There were no windows but the concealed lighting was at just under a comfortable 2000 degrees Kelvin which was lower than the temperature of the light outside the building. The furniture was Swedish. Simple and beautifully made. A desk with three telephones. A long table with six matching chairs. Two leather armchairs and a row of metal filing cabinets. His mail lay unopened on the blotter on his desk.

Howard Rogers was forty-two, born and brought up in a pleasant cabin on the shores of Lake Champlain in Vermont. He had several different medical qualifications but his expertise as a psychiatrist was the talent for which he had been moved to the small base in Florida, about forty miles up the coast from Tampa and St Petersburg. He had had several quite intense affairs but he had never married or seriously considered it. For him it was his work that mattered. He was privileged to carry out medical experiments that would otherwise be rated as not only irresponsible but patently illegal.

He had written several studies on the effects of drugs on different personalities which had been published in the appropriate scientific journals but the publication of the studies based on his main work had been vetoed by the people in Washington who employed him. He had never served in the US Army and his military rank was only to give him the status to carry out his work without interference.

He had two assistants who were medically qualified and a confidential secretary. A male secretary. The fact that he was unmarried and had a male secretary meant that he was the subject of much ribaldry among the military men at the base and there were some who said that he was obviously queer. Neither the jokes which came back to him nor the suspicions of his fellow officers offended him in any way. He was too familiar with the vagaries of the human mind to be offended or resentful.

Now that his contract had been renewed for a further two years he was negotiating the rental of a pleasant cabin a few miles north at Bayport.

Army Medical Supply Depot 77 was responsible for the testing, storing and distribution of the more complex or sophisticated drugs in current use by the US Army. There was a staff of just over two hundred, half of them pharmacists and the others stock-keepers and administrators including specialists in transport. There was an air-strip at the far side of the installation with hangars for the two small planes and a helicopter that were maintained and operated by a group of civilians under contract to the Pentagon.

Rogers' chain of command was to the CIA at its Langley HQ. He sometimes wondered if his elaborate chain of deception was not more of a giveaway than a protection. With his high-security quarters, his independence from the military hierarchy at the unit and his total lack of response to questions as to 'what the hell' he was doing, made him more noticed and observed than was desirable. But Rogers knew that he would put up with any conditions. He was working in an area of science that was unknown territory. He was exploring the human mind. Not the human brain. That was already part of the medical encyclopaedia. But the mind, that indefinable engine of human behaviour, had always been a taboo area for anything beyond deduction and speculation. So far as he knew, and he accepted that it was an area of high secrecy, he was the only man on this earth who knew how to control the human mind. Because his masters were who they were his experiments had been in a limited spectrum of the human mind. But there was a euphoria from knowing what he knew that was like being on a permanent high from some undiscovered drug. He looked at his watch. Delgado would be with him in less than an hour. The ground staff had been assembled at the air-strip.

Rocky Delgado was Rogers' liaison man with the CIA for all the practical aspects of his experiments and Delgado had agents in the Tampa area who did the leg-work. Rogers supplied the list of characteristics they had to work to. Rogers had the final say.

The file that lay open on the table had about five or six pages. Rogers read it through and then looked at Delgado.

'Let's just go through it. Item by item.'

Delgado shrugged. 'OK. His name's Helder. Piet Helder. Dutch background. Aged 29. Works here on the site as a clerk. He checks the package before it goes to dispatch. Speaks German and Dutch. No education beyond high-school.'

'What hold would we have on him?'

'He smokes pot and keeps a supply in his quarters.'

'How do we explain why he's away for several days?'

'We induce symptoms of diabetes. He has to go for medical checks in Tampa.'

'Lifestyle?'

'Single, hetero, several girl-friends, none steady. Feckless, always in debt, plays jazz piano in clubs in Tampa and Saint Petersburg. They say he's good. Could make a living at it but is unreliable. Turns up only when he feels like it.'

'What about the pot habit?'

Delgado shrugged. 'Average, not in deep.'

'Other drugs?'

'No. None.'

'Parents?'

'Killed in a car crash three years ago.'

'Other relatives?'

'None in this country so far as we know.'

'Criminal record?'

'One indictment for possession of pot. No prosecution, no restrictions.'

'Sex?'

'Average. Takes it when it's offered. Doesn't go hunting for it. All amateurs. Girls who go for his piano-playing.'

'Friends?'

'None we would classify as friends but plenty of casual. He's not outgoing. Rather a loner.'

'When do you want to use him?'

'Soon as you fix him up.'

'What are you going to use him for?'

Delgado hesitated, then said. 'Are you sure you need to know?'

'Not if you're satisfied that he'll be able to do what you want.'

'I am, chief.'

Rogers tried not to wince. He loathed men who called people 'chief'. But he thought for several moments before he replied.

'Can you fix things with the military on the site here?'

'Tell me what you've got in mind.'

'Have a dental check. Two or three people. Just routine. But I do Helder.'

'No problem.'

'How's the girl?'

Delgado smiled. 'She's doing fine. No problems. She's had three assignments. Went like clockwork. Still doing her strip act around the bases.'

'Remember what I said. Don't keep her on the second personality for longer than ten days.'

'What would happen if we did?'

'She'd come unglued and I'm not sure I could put her together again.'

'Three days is what we've been doing.'

'That's OK.' He paused. 'How do you keep tabs on her so you can contact her?'

Delgado smiled but looked a bit shifty. 'That's "need to know category". If you felt you did need to know, have a word with Langley.'

'Who, at Langley?'

'Sutherland. D'you know him?'

'Yeah.'

'Can I ask you a question?'

Rogers said, 'Try me?'

'Why the dental check?'

'What dental check?'

'On Helder?'

'Oh that,' Rogers said leaning back in his chair. 'Well I check his teeth and find that there's quite a lot of root canal work that needs doing. And for that he'll need an anaesthetic. Then I can wave my magic wand.' He paused. 'How about I ask you a question?'

'Go ahead.'

'Now we've got Gorbachev telling us about *glasnost* and *perestroika* what have you chaps got to replace the Soviets?'

Delgado smiled. 'Well, the problem is that the *Washington Post* seems to have got Gorby's message, but the guys in Dzerdhinski Square don't seem to have taken it on board.' He paused. 'They're still playing games.'

Rogers stood up. 'How soon can you fix the dental checks?'

'I'll fix them now before I go back.'

'Will they cooperate?'

Delgado smiled and shrugged. 'They don't have any choice. Anyway they'll see it as routine.'

The phone rang and Rogers took the call. Delgado watched Rogers as he seemed to be disturbed. He heard him say, 'When have you got in mind . . .' he listened, '. . . Delgado's with me now.' He paused again, listening.

'OK. I'll tell him. Cheers.'

Rogers turned to look at Delgado. 'Brodsky's on his

way down here. He wants to see us both. Says it's very important. He'll be staying the night.' He paused. 'What's he like?'

'Tough, ambitious and contacts everywhere. I'd put my silver dollar on him being Director CIA before he's finished.'

Chapter Nineteen

———◆———

Rogers and Delgado stood in the evening shadow of the main hangar and watched as the Cessna rolled to a standstill. Two men came down the flight steps, one was Brodsky and the other was a much older man. Big-built and tanned, with his shirt open at the neck and the sleeves rolled up.

Delgado said softly, 'Christ. The big fella is Joe Maguire. Senator Maguire. Now what?'

Delgado did the introductions and led the party back to the MK Ultra offices. The Senator endeared himself to Rogers by stopping to admire the white MG. He turned to look at Rogers and Delgado.

'Who does this belong to?'

'Me, sir.'

'A discerning man, Mr Rogers. I envy you.'

Delgado looked at Brodsky. 'You said you wanted a meeting. Shall we have sandwiches while we talk?'

Brodsky looked at the Senator who said, 'Suits me. Let's get on with it.'

Rogers had phoned the officers' mess and fifteen minutes later they were sitting around Rogers' conference table with several plates of sandwiches and two large Thermos flasks.

The Senator looked across the table at Delgado and Rogers and said, 'I've got to tell you guys that MK Ultra is gradually being wrapped up.' He paused. 'You must know without me telling you that we've been operating on the very edge of the law. And often enough beyond the edge.' He sighed. 'There are politicians of both parties who have never approved of it and now that we can't quote the cold war as our reason for existence they've closed in on us.

'Unofficially I have represented the interests of MK Ultra for quite a long time. But I have to tell you that I can no longer successfully defend the operation.' He paused. 'To avoid a lot of valuable and respectable people, including me, from going to jail it's been agreed that no action will be taken against us provided MK Ultra is closed down in the next six months or so.'

Rogers said, 'Who are the bastards who are doing this to us, Senator?'

'Oddly enough they're not bastards. Many of them are men I respect. Of course, there are some who just want to settle old scores and some who would do anything to get another couple of votes.' He paused. 'But we should be making a great mistake if we didn't recognise the facts.' He paused again. 'We have ignored the laws of the land and the constitution. I won't enlarge on our sins because they were committed for a good and unselfish reason – to defend democracy and to fight back against the terrible weapons that are used by our enemies.' He shrugged. 'And that, gentlemen, is all I have to say officially.'

'Then what?'

Brodsky intervened. 'I'll deal with it from this point on and I want to thank the Senator for all that hard back-room work that he's done over the years to keep us going against a lot of opposition.'

The Senator stood up. 'I'll leave it in your good hands, Charlie.' He nodded at the others, 'Goodbye, gentlemen.'

There was a bare murmur of response and Brodsky said, 'Rogers. Show the Senator to his room.'

When Rogers came back Brodsky looked from one to the other. 'The Senator has the reputation of being an honest man and you heard what he told you about closing down MK Ultra.' He paused. 'He's also a patriotic American with strong views on our inability to strike back at our enemies because we stick by the rules of a democracy. We make threats and impose sanctions that our enemies ignore. Blow up a US embassy, kill a couple of hundred civilians and there'll always be that handful of vultures who'll relish helping you avoid the effect of any sanctions.' He paused. 'We didn't start the mind-control game. That was the Chinese and the Koreans but once again we've been stopped by the enemies within the walls. Aided of course by the commies and lefties in our own ranks.' He paused. 'They think they've stopped MK Ultra but, believe me, that ain't necessarily so.' He looked at the two men opposite. 'It depends on what you two feel about MK Ultra.' He paused. 'Delgado, how would you feel about continuing the operation if I could keep it going in some other form?'

Delgado shrugged. 'Tell me more. How do we close it down and still keep it going?'

'We move it out of the USA so that we are not subject to US laws and the constitution.'

'Then we'd lose our independence to some other country.'

'Let me explain what we've got in mind.'

Rogers noted the 'we' and realised that it wasn't as 'off the cuff' as it had sounded.

'There is a large airfield installation at a place called Mildenhall in the UK. It's shared by the Royal Air Force and the US Air Force. Our part is treated as United States territory while the agreement lasts. It's worked very well for a long time.' He paused. 'We'd move in there.'

'Who would be in charge?'

'Overall I'd be in charge but most of my time I'd be in Langley. In the UK you and Rogers can carry on as you have been doing. Rogers in charge of what I'll call the medical side and you in charge of using and controlling Rogers' patients.' Brodsky looked across at Rogers. 'I'll want you to take on staff to allow you to extend your experiments including the drugs.' He turned to look at Delgado, 'and you can increase your staff. Another junior controller and a couple of "gophers" for transport and facilities.' He paused. 'What do you think? Both of you?'

'When would the new set-up start?'

'As soon as you're ready.'

Rogers said, 'Do we really have a choice? Could I back out right now if that's what I wanted?'

'Of course. It's up to you.'

Delgado said quickly, 'You can count me in.'

'Me too,' Rogers said. 'Could be a very interesting time.'

'Think about it and confirm it with me by noon tomorrow –' he looked at his watch '– or today I guess it is.'

The next day they had both confirmed their agreement and already had names of possible recruits. Brodsky gave them both a free hand and they agreed to be ready for their own moves in a couple of months' time. Brodsky would see them settled into their new quarters and make the appropriate introductions.

Chapter Twenty

———◆———

Neither Rogers nor Delgado had families or relationships that prevented them from responding readily to the need to collect up their belongings ready for transfer to England.

At Mildenhall Brodsky had supervised the sub-dividing of the premises allotted to the combined unit. There was more space available than they needed so Brodsky had been generous with his layout.

Rogers was the top priority and he had provided a general area, six good-sized interview cubicles, accommodation for two nurses and four general assistants including a driver. Rogers' own accommodation was separate and consisted of a good-sized apartment with three bedrooms, modern kitchen and facilities rooms and a small private office space.

Delgado was allotted three sound-proof interview cubicles and several offices. His living accommodation was a slightly smaller version of Rogers' apartment. The two living quarters were both separated from the work areas and from one another.

The buildings were mainly Swedish wood structures. Clean and double-glazed and with heavy insulation. Access was by Mark X smart-cards and dead-bolt locks. There were video surveillance cameras on all three buildings.

The furniture for both office use and home use was new and again Swedish. Plain natural wood, glass and chrome.

Other necessary items for work were arriving with Delgado and Rogers on the plane.

Charlie Brodsky intended to have his wife and young daughter over in Mildenhall during the stages when he would be in the UK to supervise the operation. Four years in the Marines had got them used to frequent moves but the years in the CIA had been more stable. He didn't like his teenage daughter having to change schools and college but he was determined that they should stick together as a family.

His six years as an agent had left him with new prejudices and a number of scars on his body. He had been given the task of at least going through the motions of closing down MK Ultra. With typical caution he had put a dozen or so people in alternative jobs and about the same number under an early retirement with full pension. All the records of the project had been transferred to fiche and to CD ROMs. All the originals had been sealed in lead-lined containers and buried in the ruins of an abandoned mine not far from Pittsburgh. Two retired agents had done the physical work and supervised the burial and handed over duplicate fiches and CD ROMs to Brodsky himself, who had put them in a plastic container under the workbench of his large greenhouse where he produced big crops of Gardeners' Delight tomatoes which his wife sold from a table at the side of the road that the tourists used on their way to Lake Champlain near their house in Vermont.

Brodsky had spent time getting to know the senior RAF and USAF officers who were in charge of the huge base. He was determined to do everything possible to keep the remnants of MK Ultra alive and operative.

After his years at Langley he found it strange to be among several thousand servicemen and not know a single one of them. It was good for security but he missed the comradeship of like-minded people.

He had spent a lot of time deciding who he should choose to carry on the operation but Delgado and Rogers had been the obvious choices. They had been successful operators and they had no ties back to the States and no relationships that would be a hindrance.

Rogers was a fully qualified doctor specialising originally in the use of hypnotism to investigate the stories of people who claimed to have been involved in visitations by aliens or UFOs. He had been noticed by the CIA and recruited to investigate the possibility of mind-control which was being claimed to be used by the Chinese and the Koreans. Rogers was compensated financially for the fact that his work could not be published, but he was so successful in his work that there was no chance that he would give it up. There was nowhere else where he would be allowed to carry out the experiments that he had developed.

Brodsky respected Rogers but found him aloof and

cold. But these were virtues in the kind of work that Rogers was doing. There was no doubt that Rogers knew more about the human mind and its control and abuse than anyone else in the USA. Another characteristic of Rogers was his clinical attitude to his girl-friends. And he had many. He had a habit of offering them to anyone who was interested when he no longer wanted them.

Delgado he understood much better. Tough, independent, and an easy-going socialiser. Again very attractive to young women who saw him as the great protector and flirt. Which he was, of course. But Delgado was not the marrying kind and deceived nobody on that score. His girls were usually young shop assistants and waitresses. Plump and pretty and looking for a good time. But the girls who really went for Delgado were college girls who found his indifference fascinating. Brodsky had heard two of Delgado's girls discussing him at a party and he had agreed with the summing up of the one who laughed as she described him as being 'loving but not affectionate'.

If they were successful in this trial operation he had his list of others he could call on but he knew it would take time for any significant results. But Rogers had had to spend most of the changeover with bringing his hypnosis specimens back to normality. Or as near as he could get them to normality.

Brodsky looked at his watch. He'd go across to the officers' mess, have a quick bite and then come back to bed. He had got to be up early the next morning to meet Delgado and Rogers.

When he got back he phoned his wife and chatted for a few minutes. All was well at the other end. As always, because of habit, he laid out his clothes as for an army inspection as he undressed slowly. He read Irwin Shaw's *Girls in their summer dresses* for ten minutes before he switched off the light. Irwin Shaw was OK. He'd been a soldier in World War II.

Chapter Twenty-One

Adam Kennedy was an elegant man in his fifties. From a wealthy family whose fortune was built up from lumber-jacking grandfathers to big-scale farmers with thousands of acres, a dozen different crops and the best breeding herd of both beef and dairy stock. But Adam was edged towards the law, which he practised for several years and was admired for his subtle arguments. Eventually the subtle arguments led him to teaching. He was one of Yale's most popular lecturers on 'The philosophy of politics'. Inevitably his attractive appearance and his sharp arguments made him welcome on many TV political talk shows.

The network had just contacted Swenson who had said that in his opinion Maguire wouldn't be interested in debating 'The meaning of democracy and freedom' with anybody, including Adam Kennedy.

But when Kennedy had phoned Maguire direct he realised that Maguire hadn't even been told about the programme.

'It was meant to be a discussion rather than a debate.'

'What was the subject?'

'Roughly democracy and freedom. What are they and what are they worth?'

'Sounds more like your backyard. I'm no philosopher.'

'That's not true. I heard you on a radio programme a couple of months ago and what you said was basic philosophy.'

'What did I say?'

'You said words to the effect that a man committed to preserving free institutions can, without self-contradiction, defend them against attack from any direction whether from majorities or minorities.'

'And you reckon that's political philosophy?'

'It sure is, Senator. One can argue with it but it's what you believe in when you so frequently belabour people you think are subverting our way of life.'

'Do you disagree with that?'

Kennedy laughed. 'I disagree with almost everything that politicians say.'

'How long is the programme?'

'About thirty minutes with ten minutes taken for questions from viewers at the end. That's the usual format. The producer talked to your friend Swenson but Swenson said you wouldn't be interested. Have a word with him. We must meet some time soon anyway.'

It was a month later when Maguire made his way to the TV studio. They had included two Congressmen, one from each party, but Maguire and Kennedy were to be given most of the time.

Maguire, as always, refused to be done over by make-up and chatted to the camera crew who had just come back from filming in Bosnia. The presenter of the programme had served in the US Marines and Maguire's partiality towards ex-servicemen was amiably discussed. After the programme presenter's brief introductions the question was put to Joe Maguire.

'Senator Maguire. You have a reputation for putting the spotlight on people who you describe as enemies of democracy. What is, in your opinion, "democracy"?'

Maguire shrugged. 'The word itself is just a jargon word. What I mean by democracy is an open society whose basic requirement is that those in power are removable at reasonable intervals without violence by others with different policies.'

Maguire paused and Kennedy said his piece.

'From the point of view of political philosophers there is a flaw in that description. It implies that the desirable feature of democracy is just the election of governments by a majority of the governed.' He paused and looked at Maguire. 'What if the majority votes for a fascist or communist party which not only doesn't believe in free institutions but always destroys them when it gets into power? But if the majority of the people vote for them what do you do about it?'

'You recognise right at the start that in certain instances democrats have to act contrary to their beliefs or it will be the end of democracy itself.'

Kennedy smiled and shrugged. 'And there we have what we philosophers call "the paradox of democracy". Who has the authority to decide that a certain political party is against democracy and intent on destroying it?'

Maguire shrugged. 'You tell them by where they come from. Their roots. And there are votes and votes. Some votes are just to keep your job, others are to save your life. The Russians voted 99% for Stalin who killed more Russians than the Nazis did. The Germans voted Hitler and the Nazis into power but Hitler killed millions of people including good, decent Germans.'

The Democrat Congressman, Delillo, intervened.

'And how do we recognise these so-called subversives, Senator?'

'It's not difficult, Representative Delillo. The overt ones kidnapped and tortured 217 of our citizens in the Middle East in 1985. 690 hijackings, shootings and kidnappings. The head of the CIA station in Beirut died from his brutal treatment. The cruise ship *Achille Lauro* was hijacked off Port Said. A partially paralysed New York shop-owner was murdered and then tossed overboard still in his wheelchair.' He paused. 'Because he was a Jew. I could go on for hours, Mr Delillo. But these are just the visible operators. What worries me is the number of their supporters amongst our own population.'

Kennedy said, 'Who is to decide if these people are dangerous or not?'

'Professor Kennedy, it is the responsibility of our guardians, the US armed forces, the FBI, the CIA, the National Security Agency.'

'But who decides what is subversive?'

'Common sense and the law and the constitution. To quote the words of the constitution – "a traitor is a person who gives aid and comfort to the persons seeking to destroy our country, openly or secretly".'

The presenter said, 'We've had a lot of calls from viewers but I'm afraid we have run out of time. My thanks to our panel and for their frank speaking.'

As the lights went off and the mikes were switched off, the presenter looked around, smiling at Maguire. 'Our last caller just said, "Give the panel a message - don't mess with Texas".' Only Maguire and Kennedy had been amused.

Maguire had been impressed by Kennedy and his calm way of making his points. And when they'd spent a few minutes with the others in the hospitality room he had suggested that they had a meal together. Kennedy had heard that Maguire lived on a boat and had asked what it was like. In all Maguire's time on the boat not more than half a dozen people had been invited on board. When he suggested after their meal that they could have coffee on board, Kennedy had been flattered by the invitation.

As Maguire made the coffee in the galley, Kennedy sat with him.

'I suppose the three most beautiful things on this earth are a boat like this, a two-year-old racehorse and a very beautiful woman.'

Maguire laughed softly. 'You're obviously a romantic.' He paused. 'And you're absolutely right.'

'Changing the subject — you are obviously deeply concerned with intelligence matters and security. I don't know what committees you serve on but I recognised in what you said the exasperation, anger even, that comes to any man who has to make decisions about how far we can go in protecting our society.'

As Maguire put down the coffee-pot on the fold-down table in the galley, he said, 'How far would *you* go?'

'It sounds evasive or deceptive if I say I don't know. There are a lot of things I detest about our country and I wouldn't lift a finger to save them.'

'What things? Give me an example.'

'The power of capitalism over ordinary men's lives, the colour thing and the drug business.'

'That's not my world, Adam. I'm concerned with actual direct attempts to bring us down.' He paused. 'Let's talk about you.'

Kennedy laughed. 'The Hampshires. Not a holiday cottage. Actually born and brought up there. A very pretty wife who thinks I'm not too bad a tennis-player but I read too much.' He laughed. 'Sometimes when she says something like "you should be out in the fresh air not reading books all the time", I can hear my mother's voice.' He shrugged and smiled. 'That's about it.'

For the first time in his life Maguire knew that he had a friend. Not a pal. Not a mate. But a man who was at ease with himself and who was brighter than he, Maguire was, himself. There was an old-fashioned word that came to him. *Galant.* Like those people Louis Auchincloss and Gore Vidal write about.

Kennedy had got Joe Maguire talking about Korea and Vietnam, still seething at the memories of body-bags and insults from both draft-dodgers and the civilian population who couldn't have told you the name of the capital of either country.

It was 2 a.m. when Maguire walked Kennedy back to the road and waited for a cab. And then walked back to his boat.

In the cab Kennedy leant back and closed his eyes. He was a philosopher not a psychologist but when he thought of the m.v. *Aquila* he could recognise a womb when he saw one.

Talking with Maguire had reminded him of the quote from the book of Job – 'Shall mortal man be more just than God? Shall a man be more pure than his Maker?'

Chapter Twenty-Two

Annie Cooper knew that she was being shmoozed when Maguire suggested that their next monthly meeting should be held on the m.v. *Aquila*.

When they had settled down opposite one another in the galley with the coffee jug and paraphernalia all in place, she smiled to herself as she noticed various small masculinities like the sugar still in its paper bag, the teabags Indian not Earl Grey, and éclairs and meringues still in an open cardboard cake-box from Piece of Cake. She helped herself to sugar and an éclair, licked her fingers and searched in vain for a Kleenex.

'How do you find life on the boat?'

'Suits me fine, honey. Peace and quiet and time to read something other than official crap.'

'I heard that you'd become very matey with Adam Kennedy these days.'

Joe Maguire laughed. 'I wouldn't say matey. Matey's not a word that sits well with our Adam.' He smiled. 'But we get on well together. He has a lot of qualities I admire.'

'Like what?'

'Like he's not a politician, he doesn't have a closed mind to anything and he means what he says.' He shrugged. 'I've got a pretty efficient bullshit detector and he passes all the tests.' He paused. 'He ain't always right but he means what he says and he doesn't grind axes.'

'Did you see the piece in the *Washington Post* last week?'

He shrugged. 'Just a fishing expedition but no other media took it up.' He sighed. 'Looks like one of your so-called committee people had planted the story.'

'Are you going to respond to it?'

Maguire smiled. 'Not personally. I wasn't actually named. But if you know who the leaker was you'd better warn him that he's walking on very thin ice.'

'Is that a threat, Joe?'

She expected him to deny it but he just shrugged and said, 'I guess you could call it that.'

'I haven't been able to provide any sort of evidence that you've been able to even reduce the scale of the operation.'

Maguire reached for a file from the brief-case beside his seat. He held it as he looked at her. 'These are operations that have been closed down in the last three months.' He handed her the file and inside was just one sheet of typed paper. She read it slowly and carefully.

Burch, Dr Neil/LSD and the Air Force: Smithsonian: Index and Institutional Notifications

Subproject 8: MKULTRA: Boston Psychopathic Hospital

Subproject 16: MKULTRA: Testing Apartment Rental

Subproject 20: MKULTRA: SynthesisDerivative of Yohimbine Hydrochloride

Subproject 44: MKULTRA: Testing of Aromatic Amines at University of Illinois

Subproject 49: MKULTRA: Hypnosis at (excised) University

Subproject 59: MKULTRA: Unwitting Drug Tests at University of Maryland

Subproject 67: MKULTRA: CIA Use of Institutes Facilities – University of Indiana

Subproject 87: MKULTRA: Hyper-Allergic Substances

Subproject 122: MKULTRA: Study of Neurokinin

Subproject 127: MKULTRA: Disaster/Stress Study

Subproject 128: MKULTRA: Rapid Hypnotic Induction

Subproject 132: MKULTRA: Safe-house – Not San Francisco

Subproject 148: MKULTRA: (1) Marijuana Research

MKSEARCH 6 – MKACTION

MKSEARCH 4 – Bureau of Narcotics Safe-house

When she had read it several times she slid the sheet back into the folder and handed it back to him.

'Can I show it to a couple of the committee people?'

'It's more than just "Eyes Only" level of security. Are there two you could trust that far?'

'Yes. You've only got to read it to realise the scale of what's been going on and to understand what would happen if it was made public.' She paused. 'It's frightening, Joe.'

'It's kept us ahead of the rest of the world in this area.'

'It's not what they've discovered about hypnosis and drugs. It's what they do with that information. It doesn't bear thinking about.'

'How long since you've been to the Arlington Cemetery?'

She looked surprised. 'Two, maybe three, years.'

'And how long since you've been to the Vietnam Memorial?'

'I've never been there, Joe. I'm not that fond of cemeteries.'

'Well, go and see it before you pick your two committee people. The Memorial was built from private funds, no public funds. There are polished black marble panels and on the panels in the chronological order of their deaths are inscribed the names of fifty thousand Americans killed in the Vietnam War. Any day you go, there will be crowds of people putting flowers and pictures of dead soldiers at the foot of the monument.' He paused and she could see that he was too moved by his thoughts to speak for a few moments. And then he said, 'That's where MK Ultra started, Annie. An attempt to see that we were never again caught in that kind of trap.' He pushed over the file. 'Take it. And care for it.'

'Are you safe alone on this boat?'

Maguire was back to his normal self as he said, 'You see the chandlery over there?'

'Yeah.'

'And the guy coiling ropes?'

'Yeah.'

'Well he's CIA and two others are ex-CIA and one ex-

Special Forces.' He smiled at her. 'They look after me, Annie. There are a couple of video cameras as well. Permanently on.'

'Don't ignore the piece in the *WP*.'

'Tell me more.'

'There are people who have vague ideas about what's going on in the CIA and one of their ways to probe is that comment in the paper. What does Senator Maguire do in his spare time? And why is he on the Senate Intelligence Committee not the Armed Services Committee? Is it true that he has an office in the CIA's HQ at Langley?'

Maguire shrugged and smiled. 'Nobody's responded. It'll die the death with all the other garbage they print.'

'There's a growing body of people who are determined to put restrictions on the CIA. Not just your part of it.'

He shrugged. 'You couldn't have better proof of the need for an effective CIA when you see the opposition to it.'

'They aren't talking of closing it down. Just curbing what they see as excess.'

'Don't give me that rubbish, Annie. You know as well as I do that somebody's got to do the dirty work to stop the bleeding-hearts from selling us down the river. And to stop them from being manipulated by those countries or governments who openly declare their enmity to the USA, but strangely enough don't find it obscene to send delegations to plead for our taxpayer's money from the pussy-cats in the State Department. Money that goes into their private accounts in Swiss banks or some goddamned Pacific island.'

Chapter Twenty-Three

It was nearly six weeks before the CIA assessment team could spare the time to evaluate Fulton's claims. But in the interval Fulton had been taken over by Dr Loomis.

Loomis was in his middle-fifties. Medically well-qualified and highly respected for his courageous experiments. He was quite secretive about his past but painted a picture of a Scottish background. To the amusement of his juniors he was given to larding his talk with small touches of Scottish words. All young men were 'laddies' and all young women were 'lassies' and inevitably babies were 'wee' and 'bonnie'.

Fulton's work with the girl had been noticed by Loomis because it bore out Loomis's theories of what he called 'depatterning', a process that was based on the work of two British psychiatrists. It was a harsh and painful process for the so-called 'patient'.

The two CIA officers who were to assess the usefulness of Loomis's theories and Fulton's actual work, were not medically qualified and not much interested in the methods used, solely in the possible usefulness of being able to use someone to carry out actions that would be considered by normal people as totally repugnant and then have the memory of what they had done totally wiped-out from their memories.

Dr Loomis operated from a small wing of a hospital that treated patients who were mentally ill but Loomis's section was completely isolated from the main buildings.

On the morning of the assessment he had walked the two CIA men through the long corridor of the unit. He was aware that the screams that came from several cubicles were disturbing the CIA men and Loomis waved his hands toward the screams dismissively.

'Some patients require electroshock treatments and a brief pain can make some folk a bit sensitive. I'll explain this when we get to my office and you meet Fulton, the psychiatrist in charge of our major operation.'

Ellis and Cooper, the CIA men, had been introduced to Fulton and coffee had been available. Ellis noticed that nobody asked for the coffee.

They sat around a small table and Dr Loomis took over.

'Let me explain what we mean when we talk about "depatterning". It starts with "sleep therapy" when we administer a kind of cocktail of drugs. Drugs including Thorazine, Nembutal, Seconal, Veronal and Phenergan. Then there is a period of electroshock treatment. Usually several days.

'When we are aiming at depatterning we normally use a female. And our aim is to move her through three stages. In the first stage the subject loses most of her memory. She still knows where she is, why she is there and who the people are who are treating her.

'In her second phase, the patient loses what we call her "spare-time images". She can't answer questions about where she is and how she got there. This leads to considerable anxiety on the woman's part. In the third stage the anxiety goes but there is complete amnesia for all former events in the patient's life.'

Loomis pointed and turned to Fulton.

'Dr Fulton will tell you about our successful operation to arrive at complete control of the woman concerned.' He nodded at Fulton.

'The subject is a young lassie who has been treated by both drugs and hypnosis. She lives a normal life and has a job. Actually in a CIA unit. In what we could call Personality A she acts perfectly normally. Under hypnosis she is, let's call it, Personality B, and in that state she will do what she is asked to do. Even things that are illegal or abnormal. And this is where we move into a more serious role where the woman in Personality B is hypnotised down to another level. Let's call that Personality C. In that state the woman will do anything she is told to do. Criminal acts, violence, anything. No restrictions. This is the stage we thought might interest your people.'

There was a long silence and then Ellis said, 'Can anyone get her into Personality B?'

'Probably. We're not sure.'

'What about Personality C?'

Fulton shook his head. 'There's only one person can get her to that stage and that's me.'

'Have you used her in that stage?'

'Yes.'

'What did she do?'

Fulton looked at Loomis who shook his head.

'We can't discuss that but we can virtually guarantee that the young woman concerned, if thoroughly briefed and trained, will do anything you ask for.'

Ellis shrugged and said, 'Take it we're interested provided the operation is approved by Langley.' He paused. 'When could we start?'

Fulton shrugged. 'Technically right now, but you'll have to allow for a very thorough briefing if it involves extreme measures.'

'Could we see the woman? Not formally. Just passing by.'

Loomis looked at Fulton, then said, 'No problem, but don't stare at her or speak to her.'

Ellis stood up. 'Thanks for putting us in the picture. You'll hear direct from Langley. Probably tomorrow.'

In the car on the way back to Langley Ellis said, 'Good-looking broad. D'you think that Fulton guy is screwing her?'

Cooper shrugged. 'I'd say he was gay.' He didn't sound interested.

'Who pays those guys?'

'We do. Most of it's from CIA Special Operations Funds.'

'D'you think Langley will OK it?'

'I'd bet the ranch that they've already OK'd it. You know them. We're just another security barrier.'

'You got any ideas on how to use her?'

'Yeah. Have you?'

'The guy at the National Security Agency at Fort Meade. We know he's getting money from the KGB guy and we know he's up-dating them on Grade 2 encryption. But we can't prove it. And yours?'

'The CIA guy in Berlin who's playing footsie with the East Germans.'

Ellis laughed. 'Why not do them both?'

Chapter Twenty-Four

Johnny Fulton was not a car buff but he was a little bit proud of his immaculate white Mustang and as he loaded his kit and the girl's luggage into the boot he decided to check the tyre pressures and the oil level. All was well and despite the early start it was warm enough to have the canvas hood down. He was vaguely aware that it epitomised the usual fantasy of a beautiful convertible with a pretty girl beside him in the passenger seat. And it wasn't a long journey to Fort George Meade, a thousand-acre site that accommodated the NSA. The National Security Agency.

Most Americans can give a reasonable description of the role of the FBI and the CIA. The FBI is crime-busting and the CIA is something to do with spies. Few could give a vague description of what the NSA does. They would be surprised to learn that the NSA was the jewel in the crown of the United States espionage and security organisations. It was, in fact, the largest espionage organisation in the free world.

What had started in a small back room was now virtually a city with a resident population of 3500 which became
nearer to 60,000 when the nine-to-five commuters turned
off the Baltimore-Washington Parkway into the sprawl of
twenty buildings that housed and served its highly skilled
employees. It has its own power supply and a shopping
mall that can provide most of its inmates' needs from a
haircut to banking, cosmetics, books and a police force. It
even has its own TV station and studios. Locally and in
the intelligence community it is known as SIGINT City.

There were several disadvantages to being an employee
of the NSA. The first was that your background, character,
associates and finances would be explored very thoroughly
by assessment specialists. The second was that it was
totally forbidden to talk to anyone outside the agency
about any aspect of the NSA. The security embraced everything from stochastic maths to the brand of toilet rolls
used in the wash-places. It didn't matter whether you were
a mathematical genius or a cleaning lady, if you were found
to break the rules there was no warning – you were out
within an hour of the assessments committee's decision.
Which usually took not more than an hour from the
discovery of the breach of contract to action.

If asked officially what the NSA did for a living, the
official answer was both accurate and deceiving. The NSA
was a government organisation that supervised radio and
telephone communications. A very modest description of
its role in the defence of the USA.

Put more crudely, NSA monitored all radio and telephone traffic in the whole world. Whether that traffic was
highly encoded or in clear.

At the same time that an NSA system might be monitoring a Russian Major giving instructions to his tank squadron regarding the move to Moscow, another unit might be eavesdropping on a French treasury minister discussing the take-over of a major oil company. Nothing escaped the ears of the NSA. The claim was not subject to exceptions or breakdowns. NSA simply did what it was required to do and with no remit to ask the reason why. It cost just over 2000 dollars a day to shred and then burn the rolls of computer print-out that had been checked for key words and cleared of significance. But almost five per cent of what was preserved would warrant classification of 'eyes only'. Although they would never admit it, NSA sometimes passed on commercial or negotiating information to American companies. It was against the protocol, but who could condemn when their accusers themselves couldn't prove what went on. Foreign governments through their diplomats complained that the NSA was guilty of commercial espionage and they were courteously asked to provide evidence. NSA insisted that if ever such action was proven heads would roll. Sometimes, when the accusations were too near the bone, it was heads at the commercial organisation that rolled. Government contracts were powerful weapons.

It was only twenty-two miles from Washington to Fort George Meade through the pleasant Maryland countryside, but Fulton had stopped halfway for him and the girl to have coffee at a diner. He wanted her to be totally relaxed for the meeting. Only two other people knew about the operation and they were both senior CIA but not part of MK Ultra. All they wanted was a successful conclusion, but he had to let her see the target in his normal environment at NSA. He had been under surveillance for nearly six months but his KGB controller was an experienced operator. They had no doubts that the target was guilty of treason but they were far away from being able to produce evidence that would stand up in court. Meantime, there were the continued leaks of high-security information passing to Moscow. And nobody really wanted the revelations that would be inevitable in a court-case. Operation Karla could be the solution of a lot of internal problems. It had taken a lot of hard work to get the girl to this level of control. Originally it had been planned to hand her over to a CIA agent already under control but it became obvious that without himself in control it wouldn't work and the girl became uneasy so he had to take over the whole operation. The briefing had been meticulous and had taken nearly a month before he was satisfied that they could go ahead. The visit to the NSA was solely so that she could recognise the target in his normal surroundings. She had seen photographs. Grainy black-and-white shots and a couple of minutes of video tapings of him getting into his car. She had no idea of why she had to be able to recognise the man away from the NSA. The training at the firing-range had been sold as a standard requirement for her promotion.

He could see the ten-storey block of the NSA building as he turned off onto Savage Road. Two men who looked like FBI agents checked their credentials at the guard-room at the entrance to the ten-foot high Cyclone fence with its multiple rows of barbed wire. They were escorted at walking pace through the gates in the next fence of high-voltage wire, and then one further Cyclone fence with closed circuit television cameras. The US Marine showed them their slot in the visitor's car-park and ordered Fulton to leave the car unlocked and hand over the keys. He checked on Fulton's key-ring that there was no spare key for the car.

There were a dozen wide, stone steps to the only guard-house that led directly into the main building. Here they were issued with computer-chipped security badges which were pinned to them by a Federal Protective Service Guard in a blue uniform. After an escorted walk down a maze of corridors that seemed to have been designed to confuse rather than assist, they were shown into a window-less room with air-conditioning and comfortable chairs. Dr Townsend who received them seemed a little puzzled at their brief programme.

'And all you want is for the young lady to see O'Hara in his work environment. Do you want to talk to him at all?'

Fulton shook his head. 'No thanks. Just the sighting is enough.'

'Can I ask you what this is all about?'

Fulton smiled. 'I can't give you any more information, sorry.'

'Well you've got high-class credentials.' He sighed and shrugged. 'Our's not to reason why.'

'I'll be coming with you both,' Fulton said. 'Shouldn't take more than five minutes or so.'

Dr Townsend looked at the girl. 'You ready to go, miss?'

She nodded. 'Yeah.'

They were back in the meeting room fifteen minutes later with coffee and sandwiches. Fulton and Townsend chatted about the talents of Art Tatum compared with those of Duke Ellington, then it was time to leave and Dr Townsend escorted them back to stage 1 of their departure, shook hands with both of them and wished them luck in whatever they were doing. It took nearly an hour before Fulton was handed back his car keys in exchange for his and the girl's computerised identity badges. It took another fifteen minutes before they were through the Cyclone fences and back onto the highway.

As she saw the signs she said, 'The sign was showing Baltimore.'

'That's where we're going. That's where O'Hara lives.'

'Are we going to meet him?'

'I'll explain when we've booked in at the motel.'

She shrugged and was silent. She had learned the ground rules in the last few weeks.

At the motel he had used his mobile to contact his observer-contact at the NSA. They had been given a secure frequency but they talked cautiously.

'Checking Bing.'

'Acknowledge Blue Eyes. All on timetable here. Over.'

'My need still three hours approx.'

'No problem. Over.'

'Over and out till soon.'

He sat on the bed and unwrapped the gun from the oily cloth and wiped it dry with Kleenex. She had chosen it herself. A Hekler and Koch P7 with just a single chamber loaded with Smith and Wesson P7 M 10 5 cartridges. It was a superior weapon developed especially for use by law enforcement units. He checked it carefully and then put it inside one of the Nike trainers in his hand luggage. The clipboard and the magazines he left on the chair beside his bed.

He paid in advance for both rooms for a week and got a receipt. Back in his room he began to feel the tension of what he was about to do. If it went wrong it would go wrong in a big way. God knows where it would end. But if it went to plan then he would be remembered for having found a new and devastating weapon for the CIA's armoury.

He knocked on her door and walked in to her room. She was sitting on the bed, watching TV. He looked at his watch. There was plenty of time and he didn't want the Karla personality around for too long. When she got worked up she could be too aggressive. He looked at the window. It was already getting dark and there was an hour before O'Hara would get back to his pad.

He went over the photographs of O'Hara with her and the dialogue with the clipboard and the magazines and then put her through the change to Rosie. No problem.

Half an hour later she was Karla and helping load their kit into his car. Whether it worked or not they wouldn't be coming back to the motel.

O'Hara's place was one of a huddle of wooden buildings that were raised on stilts to provide space for cars to be parked underneath them, and the house itself was reached by a wooden staircase that gave onto a verandah that was big enough to take a couple of chairs and a small table for use in fine weather.

To park the car so that they could leave quickly, he had to keep turned in his seat to watch O'Hara's place.

There were lights in both windows and it was beginning to rain as he watched her making her way up the stairs. He saw O'Hara open the door and the girl showing him the magazines. For a moment O'Hara hesitated and then he invited her in. Fulton had reckoned on a maximum of fifteen minutes and he rolled down his car window to listen for any disturbance. It was only six minutes later that he saw the lights go off and then the girl making her way down the wooden stairs. She didn't look across to the car and was obviously intent on coping with the hazards of the rough stairway.

On the ground she behaved exactly as he had drilled her, walking carefully, in no hurry to reach the car.

He switched on the engine and checked that the muddy driveway was clear as she settled in the passenger seat and then headed back to the highway and the signs that pointed to Washington DC.

He said quietly. 'Tell me.'

'Tell you what?'

'How it went for God's sake.'

'No problem. He obviously wanted to screw me so he asked me in saying he'd like to see the boating magazine.' She paused. 'I shot him as he looked at it.'

'Where did your shot go?'

'Just above his nose. He fell back on the bed and I picked up the magazines and the clipboard, checked that there was no pulse, switched out the lights and left.'

She looked strangely wild and spoke with that edgy,

rasping voice that she always had when she was Karla.

'And you think it all went to plan?'

'Too fucking true, buddy, too fucking true.'

Ten minutes later he pulled into a truckers' stopover and got her back to Rosie and then to Joanna Page who said she was hungry. He took her back to his place and gave her a drink before taking her to the Hilton for a late dinner. As she drank in the sitting-room he took the gun, the magazines and the clipboard and shoved them in the wardrobe in his bedroom.

The following day there was no mention in the media of a murder in the Baltimore area but the day after there was a brief paragraph about a government employee shot and killed in his own home. The Baltimore Police Department were pursuing their enquiries. At the moment it was considered as 'murder by a person or persons unknown'. Fulton had no twinge of conscience when he breathed a sigh of relief as he read the piece.

Charlie Brodsky himself de-briefed him. Charlie didn't like the sound of it. It sounded too easy.

'How did she know he was dead?'

'She checked his pulse. I'm satisfied he was dead.'

'Have you talked with her about this?'

'No. Except for de-briefing her right after it happened.'

'Have you got any objection to a trained de-briefer talking to her?'

'Personally I've no objection but she won't remember anything of what went on. If she did then we'd be in the shit.'

'So tell me again. You hypnotised her and called her Rosie and while she's still hypnotised you hypnotise her from Rosie to Karla. Why the double dose?'

'An extra layer of security, and Karla's a very different personality. Rosie wouldn't do what we wanted. Karla will. She's as tough as any man.'

'Did the NSA people help you?'

'They weren't informed but I had some unofficial help from inside. But the person didn't know what it was all about.'

'Can she ever find out what you've been doing with her?'

'No. Only I know the final password that makes the last personality change.' He smiled. 'Even you don't know it.'

'And if you get knocked down by a bus?'

Fulton shrugged. 'The password never gets used again, so no problem.'

'How often could you do this sort of thing?'

'Provided it was worth the risk, I guess we could do it once a month.'

Charlie Brodsky looked across at Fulton.

'Thanks for your hard work and thanks for what you got done. The bastard was covered too well for any legal action. He deserved what he got.' He paused. 'I'll think about the next move and contact you. Have some leave for God's sake.'

As Fulton made his way back to his office he felt tired and depressed. He had done something, maybe two things, that nobody had ever done before so far as he knew and there was no one to share the triumph with him. Ordinary people would think he was either evil or crazy. He wondered what sort of deal he could do with Charlie Brodsky if he resigned. They would have to be generous because he knew so much. He was two hours down the south coast road before he realised that Brodsky did have an alternative. He didn't *have* to be generous. He could be ruthless instead. Just call it a day and nobody would be any the wiser. Nobody even to pick up his pension rights. And no name on the marble plaques at Arlington Cemetery.

A month later he and the girl were in Berlin staying at the Remtor Hotel not far from the Zoo. Way back in Pittsburg the pistol had been tossed into the open cupola of molten metal at an iron foundry and a second later it no longer existed. At least a thousand bucks, Fulton thought, even second-hand.

Chapter Twenty-Five

Despite Maguire's dislike of what he called 'socialising' there were inevitably occasions when he had to attend luncheons or dinners for the sake of CIA diplomacy, but private socialising was not part of that agenda. There was only one exception and that had been having dinner quite often with Adam Kennedy and his wife Adele in their home in Georgetown. It was always just the three of them for Adam Kennedy knew that that was the only basis that Maguire would find acceptable.

It was after one of these occasions that the Kennedys were having a last glass of wine before going to bed and found themselves discussing their guest and his character.

It was Adam Kennedy who started it by saying, 'I wonder why he never married again.'

Adele smiled. 'All those years in the army have had their effect.'

'What's that mean?'

'Well, the kind of woman he needs would be put off

by the military bit. She'd probably vaguely admire it but it would discourage her.'

'You say "the kind of woman he needs". What kind of woman is that?'

She laughed softly. 'Like me. An Italian who thinks he's absolutely marvellous and just wants to make him happy.' She paused. 'He's neglected. A stray dog. Handsome, brave, a great protector and a one-woman guy.'

'So what's wrong with that?'

'Nothing. It's highly desirable but you pay a price to get in.'

'In what way?'

'All those years as a loner have put their mark on him. It'll take a lot of hard work for that dog to expect to get a pat on the back, let alone a gentle stroke.'

'Would the pay-off for all that hard work be worth it?'

'To the right woman – yes.'

'Isn't he a bit old for all that?'

'I don't think so.'

He smiled. 'Have you got someone in mind?'

She laughed softly. 'Vaguely.'

'Who?'

'I'll think about it.'

'What do you think is Joe Maguire's biggest virtue?'

'For me it's all wrapped up in the same thing. He's got a big ranging mind. He would make a great President because he has never been in routine politics. But I guess what I value most is his complete honesty. He says what he thinks. He even openly changes his mind if somebody else's argument convinces him.'

'Not a great catch as a lover.'

She laughed. 'All the same he reminds me of you.'

'In what way for heaven's sake?'

'The only difference between you is that you are better educated than he is, but he can counter that with having been successful in so many fields – could have been pro-footballer, was exceptional soldier, not a bad lawyer and these days it looks like he's doing something useful for what I guess is the CIA.'

For a few moments he sat there, silent, and then he stood up, holding out his hand.

'Time for bed, honey.' But as she stood up he put his arms around her and kissed her before he released her to open the curtains and look at the scattered lights of the city winking sleepily as the autumn fog turned it all into the kind of scene that French films always seem to start with. It was heavy clouds and rain on slippery wet cobble-stones.

As he undressed his mind was still on what Adele had said. Such a shrewd analysis of Joe Maguire but with an entirely different appreciation of the man. He wondered if the rumours he'd heard about a committee being put together to destroy Joe Maguire was likely to get off the ground. He wondered who she had in mind to provide aid and comfort for Joe Maguire. He wondered what that strange female mind had made of himself when they had first met. For him the first time that he'd seen her had been enough although these days he swore that it was her intelligence and sophistication. They had certainly played a part when he had got to know her but there was no doubt that it was her beauty that had been the prime incentive. Adele di Marco was the daughter of the then Italian ambassador to Washington. A man of great charm and amiable disposition. His daughters were both beautiful but Adele's was a quiet beauty that specially appealed to the argumentative academic.

Chapter Twenty-Six

Maguire looked across his desk at Charlie Brodsky who had recently been promoted to Deputy Director of the CIA.

'Did you see this piece in the *National Enquirer*?'

He pushed two pages torn from a magazine across his desk and sat quietly while Brodsky read it. When he'd finished Brodsky looked up at Maguire.

'Yeah. It came out a couple of weeks ago.'

'You notice the headline?'

Brodsky looked at the pages and read out loud. 'Who is playing God with Americans' lives?' He looked at Maguire. 'This is from a so-called investigation of Hadlow Rehabilitation Centre, which is perfectly legit and official and solely concerned with ex-service personnel with mental problems claimed to be due to trauma from witnessing active service incidents during war service.'

'It talks about hypnotising them, Charlie.'

Brodsky shrugged. 'First of all, Joe. It's nothing to do with Ultra or any other CIA operation. It's solely run by armed service doctors.' He paused. 'Sometimes they use hypnotism to try and find the root cause of mental fixation.'

'So why does the article state that it's done by the CIA and without the patient's agreement?'

'Joe. Those bastards would swear it was done by the President himself to get what they call an exposure. And the poor wretches who find themselves in the Rehab unit are too sick in many cases to know what day it is.' He paused. 'These are still men who can't forget things they saw in Vietnam or in Germany.' He sighed. 'The Navy has a place too and so does the USAF.'

'Does anyone get cured?'

'I think so. Maybe not cured but their lives made more tolerable. Why don't you pay them a visit?'

'I'm told that there's some Senator asking for a special committee to look into the whole territory of the CIA. Have you heard anything?'

'It's one of those bits that float around looking for a home from time to time.'

'Who's the Senator stirring it up?'

Brodsky shrugged. 'It's usually Heller. Worried that nobody's even heard of him. I'll let you have his CV. Went to Canada to dodge the draft way back and claimed deafness to avoid any kind of prosecution. Said to be a first-class lawyer but vindictive in questioning. Juries don't like it. An asshole but a clever one.'

'What's this problem you've got in the UK?'

'I'm trying to avoid a clash of egos and I'm not sure how to deal with it.'

'Tell me.'

'You remember the outfit we had down in Florida? I went with you when you told them about Ultra being run down and we gave the two guys there the choice of calling it a day with compensation or going to the place we were setting up in the UK. Just a very small operation. They both opted to make the move to the UK. One was Rogers, a very bright medic, a psychiatrist, and he was to look after that side of it. The other was a CIA-trained guy named Delgado. He arranged the use of the people who Rogers had under his control.'

'What kind of control, Charlie?'

'Straight hypnotism most of the time.'

'Tell me more.'

'They worked here together, each looking after his own bit. Rogers supplying what Delgado needed and Delgado using them operationally. Rogers had some idea of what they did because of what Delgado asked for, but Rogers didn't know, and wasn't interested in, what they did for Delgado. It's worked well until I had to post another couple to the UK who were getting problems in the US.

'This was a guy named Fulton and a young woman named Joanna Page.' Brodsky paused. 'These two are special and more valuable to Ultra than any others. They are being used on top-secret work under direct orders from the CIA.'

'Why are they so special?'

'Because the girl's under hypnosis that couldn't be done in any other way and nobody except Fulton is capable of controlling her.'

'And your guy Rogers thinks that he's the senior man and should be in charge of the two of them.'

'Yeah. That's about it, Joe.'

'And if one team had to be thrown away, which team would you keep?'

'Without doubt, Fulton and the Page girl.'

'If I remember reading their reports, Rogers and Delgado find it extremely convenient to be on a site, the airfield, where there are several thousand US service people who can be used if necessary.'

'Yes.'

'And the other two?'

'No. They don't recruit at Mildenhall and a lot of their practical work is in Europe.'

'So rent a place they can have as their own independent HQ.'

'It wouldn't be as secure as the place at the airfield.'

'So let Langley make it secure for you.'

'Would you speak to them about it?'

'Why so modest all of a sudden? Why don't *you* speak to them?'

'Because this team are so valuable that I need all the help I can get from Langley.'

'Does that mean you've got some opposition in Langley?'

'Not really opposition. Just people who are scared it might all come apart and they're beginning to depend on it.'

'Who shall I talk to?'

'To Rory Lewis. Just say it's about Rosie.'

The house stood well back from the road, its Victorian dark-red bricks looking less than inviting. But inside it was roomy, well-furnished and warm. The gardener came once a week and the garden itself was well laid-out. Mainly with lawns back and front with a few apple trees at the hedge that marked their land from the lush fields further on. There were seven bedrooms, three toilets, two large reception rooms divided by a sliding door. The dining-room was panelled and led to the kitchen and scullery.

It seemed a good omen that not only was the sun shining when they moved in, but there were clematis shrubs in full bloom already. And a few early lambs with the ewes in the field beyond the hedge. The house had been rented for a year with payment in advance. This had made it easier to get agreement for several modifications to be carried out to the telephone system and general security.

The two-roomed chauffeur's flat above the double garage was the base for Sgt. Logan and his monitor for the four video cameras that had been tucked into the ivy and Virginia creeper that covered most of the outer surfaces of the house.

The address was Paragon House, Smallhythe Road, Tenterden, Kent.

Tenterden was a one-main-street village on the border between Kent and Sussex. On sunny days it was definitely Sussex but most days the glamour of village shops and old buildings was washed away by its sheer, grey monotony.

From Fulton's point of view Tenterden's virtues were that both at nearby Bexhill and, in the other direction, at Ashford, there were good train services to London.

They both had Canadian passports in the name of Peter Cramer and Joan Piper. Their cover was that Peter

Cramer was a writer who needed peace and quiet for his work and frequently needed to travel in Europe.

Fulton was glad to get away from the tensions of the unit at Mildenhall. He was not a born fighter, preferring the atmosphere of laboratories and interview rooms. Apart from his own feelings, he knew that if Rogers was allowed any part in the Karla operation it would disintegrate in days. Brodsky had recognised that too, thank God, and now he could continue with the tasks that CIA Special Measures had discussed with him. His track record for them with the girl meant that he had the final say on stopping or starting a new operation.

Fulton looked out of the front windows and watched Frazier paying off the taxi-driver. He sensed that Frazier was no more than a messenger between himself and Brodsky at Langley. He had arranged for Frazier to stay at one of the pubs overnight. The girl had taken an instant dislike to Frazier the first time they had met. He had heard on the grapevine that Frazier had been in New York and had made a cock-up of some operation and been kept on doing routine jobs because he knew too much for them to sack him.

There was always a problem with diplomatically finding something for the girl to do while they discussed either a Rosie operation or particularly anything to do with Karla. So far as the girl was concerned she didn't know anything about the whole Karla set-up. She wouldn't have believed any of it anyway. What she did as Rosie sometimes shocked her and by now the Rosie operation was more or less routine. Illegal maybe, but not like Karla where even he and Brodsky used the in-house jargon euphemisms like 'finalising', 'eliminating' and 'internal cleansing'.

Now they were at Tenterden it was easy to divert the girl to a shopping expedition to London or Tunbridge Wells on the rare occasions when Frazier was around.

Frazier had brought photographs and some video footage covering people and places in the Amsterdam job and a possible target in Paris. Fulton never discussed or touched on any operational details. Frazier just brought him the results of the leg-work that others had done. And Frazier knew, without being told, that the girl was used in some way and he surmised that it was almost certainly under hypnotism.

Fulton took his colleague for a last drink at the pub and it was then that Frazier had said, 'Strange girl that Joan. Is she any good?'

'She's two CIA grades above you, my friend, and it's agin the rules to discuss CIA personnel unless it's in committee.'

Frazier laughed. 'That's one rule nobody ever sticks to.'

'They do here. A last Scotch?'

'No thanks.' He paused. 'Why so touchy?'

'Because if you had half her guts you wouldn't be a messenger boy for Langley.'

Frazier shrugged and smiled and assumed that Fulton must be sleeping with the girl.

Chapter Twenty-Seven

The three of them, Adele, Adam and Joe Maguire were sitting around a coffee table and when the phone rang Adam stood up and walked to the sideboard where the telephone and a fax machine were plugged in to a wall socket.

He picked up the phone.

'Kennedy speaking.'

'It's Angela. I'm stuck at the airport and I need to find a hotel for the night. They're all booked up. Can you recommend one who might take me?'

'For heaven's sake. Where are you – Dulles?'

'Yes.'

'We'll pick you up and you can stay with us as long as you want.'

'Thanks so much, Adam. I was beginning to panic.'

'Get yourself a coffee, honey. One of us will be there in about half an hour. Ciao.'

Adam looked across at his wife but she seemed to be busy talking with Joe Maguire.

'That was Angela. She's stranded at Dulles and no hotel. I've said we'd pick her up and she could stay here.'

'Of course.' Adele said as she stood up. 'I'll go. You two hang on here.' She nodded towards Adam and the Bluthner grand. 'Play him a bit of Delius. "The Walk to the Paradise Gardens".' She turned to look at Joe. 'They're walking along the river-bank – you'll love it.' She kissed her husband and hurried to the door. 'Must take a woolly sweater with me.' She smiled and waved. 'See you. Ciao.'

And as she said *Ciao* the penny dropped for Adam Kennedy. But as he poured out another Glenfiddich for them both his mind was not on Joe's praise of Scotch malt but on the thought that Angela's delay at the airport was strange.

Adele's sister wasn't the kind who needed rescuing from mild domestic crises. Angela de Marco was extremely efficient and apart from that if she had got stranded at the airport by now she'd be in some stretch limo on the way to town in the company of some handsome millionaire. For Angela de Marco was too beautiful ever to be stranded at a busy airport. She was two years older than her sister but she could have passed for late thirties if she had wanted to. But Angela didn't take what was her very great beauty at all seriously. It didn't interest her. Nevertheless part of that beauty was a calm self-assurance that left her permanently smiling and amused at men's efforts to get and hold her attention. If she had been analysed an observer would not be able to escape the evidence that Angela de Marco was a girls' girl. Not even vaguely lesbian but nevertheless happiest when with other young women. And a quite sharp sense of humour that was always softened by a smile from those big brown eyes.

At the moment Adam Kennedy would have put his silver dollar on Angela de Marco being the 'someone special' who Adele had in mind. She was usually so right about people but on this occasion he thought her perception was bizarre.

It was nearly two hours later when the two sisters returned. He could hear them laughing as they let themselves in. Adam was amazed to see Joe Maguire kissing Angela's hand when they were introduced. It wasn't that the gesture was so unusual, there was plenty of hand-kissing at the Italian embassy, but Joe Maguire's normal sign of approval of young women was to treat them like promising platoon commanders.

It was well past midnight when Kennedy drove Joe Maguire back to his boat. He helped Joe check the ropes holding the fenders and when they stood for a few moments in the galley exchanging Washington gossip Kennedy noticed the washed crockery in the sink. One dinner plate, one side plate, one tea mug, one dessert bowl and half a dozen bits of cutlery. It had all the man's life laid out in its simplicity. The army, the economy of effort with just one of everything. No photographs, no certificates, no trophies.

There was a piece in *De Telegraaf* that covered the reclamation of a body from a canal in Amsterdam. The body had been identified as an American citizen aged about forty named John Crocker. He worked in Holland and Belgium as a freelance journalist. The preliminary autopsy indicated that Crocker had died from a gunshot wound in the head that had been inflicted before immersion in the canal.

The report claimed that a police officer had suggested that there were security aspects to the killing as the dead man had once been a member of the CIA and had recently written mainly about current radar-guided missile systems.

The US embassy in the Hague had no comments to make on either the killing or the American's past connections with the CIA.

Relatives of the deceased had been contacted in Boston where the body would be sent after the final autopsy report had been completed. The woman who had rented the victim two rooms in the area of the Main Station had said that the victim was no trouble and well-behaved.

The coverage regarding Rupert Coombs was extensive. Newspapers and the TV stations had seized on the fact that the dead man was not only an American but had some sort of liaison responsibility with the BND, the *Bundesnachrichtendienst*, the German intelligence service, which turned it into a spy story right at the start.

The BND's HQ at Pullach had issued a statement that Rupert Coombs was solely concerned with routine financial records and was not engaged in any form of espionage. It was thought that the killer or killers had placed the bomb under the wrong car. It had been parked outside a local club that was patronised by a number of men who worked at BND HQ.

Fulton had read all the photocopied material that Langley had sent to him and was quietly satisfied with his and the girl's part in both operations. They had suggested that he should fly over for two or three days' discussion of the next operations but he was in no hurry to get involved in all the hassle again without a break.

The girl seemed contented enough. He was teaching her to play tennis most afternoons and chess in the evenings. Unfortunately neither he nor Langley could congratulate her on her work because she wouldn't know what they were talking about.

Senator Heller had gathered around him eight or nine Republicans. Another Senator and the rest Congressmen. Their relationship for the moment was based solely on contriving some means of destroying the reputation of Joe Maguire. There had been talk in the early days of impeachment, but Joe Maguire was not a minister, he was chairman of no government committees and had no particular allegiance to either of the main parties. When asked what the Senator was actually responsible for his spokesman said that he was responsible for liaison between the CIA and the US Army.

Heller was a vindictive man who found it necessary to loathe personally anybody he came up against. His attack on Maguire had become a virtual crusade but his colleagues were an ill-assorted lot and although they relished the idea of an impeachment of a Senator they wished that it was not Joe Maguire. Finally they told Heller that they were not only wasting their time and efforts but were perilously near turning their media contacts against them. They'd give him a month to find some hard evidence that would go towards impeachment otherwise they would call it a day.

Heller decided that the issue should be whether Maguire took his orders from the Pentagon or from Langley. He had an investigator who was frequently used by the partners in his law practice and Heller leaked the fact that an investigator was looking into 'the dubious relationship of Senator Maguire with the Pentagon and the CIA.' Who were his masters? How far did his authority run? Who appointed him? What are his duties and who does he answer to?

The CIA did a little leaking of its own. It was revealed that the investigator was not ex-FBI nor an ex-cop but a man who was in fact only a few months out from a six-year sentence for criminal conspiracy. Who, the CIA asked plaintively, would employ such a man to investigate a senior Senator? Was this what the instigator's constituents had elected him for? That statement was a not too subtle suggestion that the instigator was a Member of Congress or even of the Senate. The media, who already knew exactly who was doing what to whom, suggested possible names with the emphasis on Senator Heller who denied any knowledge of such a conspiracy and roundly condemned attacks on individuals.

As almost always with such media contrivance the attack on Joe Maguire only put up his ratings in the polls and that, because of the convoluted effects of such publicity, meant that there were even more individual appearances of Joe Maguire on talk-shows, earnest political discussions and personal interviews by such stars as Larry King and David Letterman.

Chapter Twenty-Eight

———◆———

Joe Maguire was conscious of showing off when he'd taken her to the Jockey Club for dinner. He wasn't sure that she was all that impressed but he had enjoyed himself and the food was at least a change from the cheese omelette that he would have cooked for himself.

When they took a cab back to the river and the boat it was her third visit and she made their coffee in the galley with the assurance of a regular visitor. Her brother-in-law, Adam, had been both amused and impressed that she had been allowed on board still wearing her high-heeled shoes.

'Tell me about your life in New York.'

'You mean the gallery?'

'Anything. All of it. Why photographs not paintings?'

'Not paintings for two reasons. First there are too many art galleries in New York to compete without a lot of hype, and secondly I'm not a good judge of paintings.'

'Adam told me that you wanted to be a photographer. What made you abandon it?'

'Because I'm not a good enough photographer. I wasn't

interested in processing and dark-rooms but I knew a good photograph when I saw it. But when I started the gallery I just about survived but these days a print can fetch several thousand dollars and the standard of photography has never been higher.'

She put the coffee things on a tray that she'd bought him and joined him in the saloon.

'Help yourself to sugar.'

She sat down, smoothing her skirt as she made herself comfortable.

'Does all this political sniping get you down, Joe?'

He shrugged. 'It's only politicians and the media – not real people.' He smiled. 'You just have to make sure you don't inhale.'

'What would you have liked to be – forgetting whether you've got the qualifications for it?'

He was silent for long moments and then he said, 'I don't know. I'm not good at anything, really.'

'That's both a heap of rubbish and a lot of wisdom at the same time.'

He smiled. 'Tell me more. The lot of wisdom bit.'

'You've succeeded in half a dozen different careers. Most men would be satisfied with any single one of them.'

'They're all the same thing, honey, just wearing different hats.'

'What thing.'

'Keeping this country for good ordinary people to live in. Keeping out our enemies and asking help from nobody.'

'Completely on our own. Indifferent to other nations' fates?'

'Yes. They've got to get their own Joe Maguires.' He

paused and looked at her. 'People have got to be responsible for their own deeds. If you thieve, you go to jail, and
you go to jail if you assault someone. Right now we have
God knows how many laws to tell us how to live every
moment of our lives. Laws don't prevent these things
happening. You've got to believe. Believe in the US of A.
Believe in our Constitution.' He sighed and laughed.
'Sorry, kid. I'm preaching again. It's not my line.'

'And what is your line, Joe Maguire?'

'To stop the baddies. Throw 'em out and keep 'em out.'

'Isn't that the job of the government and the FBI and
the CIA?'

'Government. What government? Just third-rate politicians with their snouts in the trough.' He paused and
shrugged. 'And all day and every day there's a group of
politicians trying to reduce the power of the FBI and the
CIA. And that's my bit. The CIA bit and the Army.
Protecting them from their and our enemies right here in
our own country.'

'What's your favourite piece of music, Joe?'

He smiled at her deliberate change of subject and was
silent for some time. She wondered if it would be Brahms
or Beethoven.

'It's a song from way back called "Long ago and far
away . . .".'

She sang softly. '*I dreamed a dream one day and now, the dream
is here beside me.*' She laughed. 'It changes key there and it's
too high for me.'

He smiled. 'And your favourite?'

She screwed up her eyes, thinking. And then she said,
'Mine's got to be Italian. It's called "Vento". It too is from

way back but I've heard Pavarotti sing it. "*Vento, vento, portami via con te . . .*" It asks the wind to carry me away up to where the stars are shining . . .' She smiled at him. 'We don't really belong in this funny old world do we . . . we two?'

'Tell me more.'

'We both set great store by our independence. And it's real independence. We don't really care about what others think about our conclusions . . .' she paused '. . . and underneath it all but never acknowledged is sometimes the wish that there was one other person who was totally committed to agree with us. Not our views, necessarily. But us as persons.'

'Tell me about your marriage and divorce.'

She shrugged. 'He was handsome, charming, a liar and as ruthless as a Mafioso when the chips were on the table. The divorce . . .' she shrugged '. . . fortunately he was an Italian and papa saw him off.'

'What's he doing now?'

'I've no idea. I haven't heard of him in nearly twenty years.'

'It must have been a terrible time.'

'It was. And time *doesn't* heal all wounds.' She smiled at him cheerfully. 'But like you I've survived and I've learned some lessons.'

'Any chance of you coming here tomorrow? I could pick you up at Adam's place.'

'OK. What time?'

'About seven be OK?'

'That would be fine.'

She leaned forward to look at him and said softly, 'Do you ever get lonely here, Joe?'

'I'm used to being alone.'

'Being alone is something else. Being lonely is realising that everything's just as you left it. Nobody's washed up or put fresh water in a glass of flowers or . . .' she shrugged '. . . that sort of thing.'

'I've never thought of it that way but I guess you're right.' He smiled. 'Something missing.'

'I admire you so much, Joe. Your conviction, your honesty and your integrity. But sometimes when I think about you I wonder if you haven't had to pay too high a price.' She waved her elegant hand around at the boat. 'This boat is so beautiful but it doesn't say "Well done" when you get back on board after a day putting your reputation on the block for something you believe in.'

'Honey, if I'd needed political support I couldn't have done the job.' He shrugged. 'I just happened to have a strange mixture of experience that was needed to do the job.' He smiled. 'Even now I don't have a job description or even an official title.' He held out his hand. 'Let's go and get you a cab.'

Brodsky had sent him a copy of a CIA report on Heller. It seemed that he was still trying to put together some sort of group that would put their names to an attempt to impeach Joe Maguire. It also seemed that they were having problems on two fronts. Firstly they were uncertain about what grounds for an impeachment they could contrive that a Grand Jury or a Congressional committee would go with. The second problem was barely mentioned but was in every one of their minds. What personal repercussions would there be from openly attacking the CIA and one of its best-known public figures.

The report went on to comment that Langley had enough on seven of the participants including Senator Heller to bring it to a grinding halt whenever they deemed it necessary. The background covered sexual, financial and bribery activities. Brodsky had put a handwritten note in the margin to suggest that Maguire kept an eye on the media in the next few days and reference to a James Ziller one of Heller's little band of plotters.

Somebody in CIA operations had called in one of his markers with his opposite number in the FBI. They had passed on the file on Ziller J. Congressman. He read it through carefully. He was one of the Washington bureau's old China hands. Used to the weasel ways of self-important nonentities from rural landscapes. He picked up the phone and dialled Ziller's office number. A female secretary answered.

'Congressman Ziller's office, how may I help you?'

'I want to speak to Mr Ziller.'

'I'm afraid he's in conference at the moment.'

'Give him my name. It's Fox. Ask him to speak to me.'

'I'll see what I can do Mr Fox but I'm afraid he's a very busy man. Hold on.'

There was a gap of several minutes and then the secretary back again.

'I gave him your message Mr Fox but I'm afraid he's completely tied up.'

'Well contact him again and tell him it's Agent Fox, Washington bureau of the FBI.'

'I see. Hold on a minute.'

Almost immediately it was, 'Congressman Ziller what can I do for you?'

'I want to talk to you about various things. Today.'

'Today. I'm afraid that's not possible.'

'I'll be at your office in about an hour.'

'Well. If you insist. I'll do my best to be here.'

'It would be wise to be there, Mr Ziller.'

And Agent Fox hung up, slid the buff file into his black brief-case, locked it and looked out of the window. It looked as if it could rain so he took his umbrella from the hat-rack.

Ziller waved him to the chair in front of his desk.

'Make yourself at home Mr Fox.' He sat down patting the arms of his chair to show his confidence.

'Now what's troubling you?'

'Miss Carole Edge . . .' Fox watched Ziller's face. 'Is she a friend of yours?'

'What name was that?'

'Carole. Carole Edge.'

'No. I've never heard of her.'

'You've been paying her approximately two thousand dollars a month for just over a year.'

'Maybe she's one of our consultants.' He smiled. 'Can't keep track of them these days.'

'Would you check that while we talk.'

'I've just remembered. Yes. Carole. She's now part of my political set-up.' He shrugged. 'We just meet from time to time.'

'For what purpose?'

Ziller looked uneasy. 'What's this all about? You don't have any right to discuss my private life.'

'I do Mr Ziller but in this case the matter arises because Miss Edge is intending to take you to court.'

'For what?'

'She said you agreed a special bonus for a particular service which she carried out twice but you refused to pay.'

'You tell her if she'll put in an invoice I'll see it's paid immediately.'

'I'm afraid it's too late for that.'

'How come?'

'She's already in touch with a journalist who will pay her a lot more for the details.'

'What's she told him?'

'The lot. She'd get at least fifty thousand bucks for the story. And maybe even more for the pictures.'

'Pictures. I never asked for pictures.'

'In these kinds of situations they'll take pictures without you knowing.'

'Have you seen the pictures?'

'Yes.' He paused. 'They were all bondage pictures and some were of the special thing with the plastic bag.'

Ziller sighed. 'Why are you telling me all this? Whose side are you on for God's sake?'

'Congressman Ziller — let's cut out the bullshit. If this stuff gets in the press, and I understand that there's more available, you'll go down the pan. I can stop this happening but the information came to the Bureau from the CIA and I gather that you and a few others are talking about taking action against the CIA.' He paused. 'Not a helpful situation.'

'It was just chat, Mr Fox. Nobody took it seriously.'

'That wasn't what I heard. Even a Senator involved. Not a good scenario for saving reputations.'

'What other reputations in the group?'

Agent Fox shook his head. 'That's confidential.'

'I'll pull out if that's what you want.'

'It could make a difference to our attitude. And to the CIA's attitude too.'

Ziller sighed. 'I'd need more assurance than that.'

'You do your part and we'll do ours but you need to get a move on or it'll be too late.'

'I'll phone them when you've gone.'

Dealing with Miss Carole Edge was no problem. She'd been through the hoops before. There was no journalist involved. He listened to the recordings of Ziller's frantic calls to the others in the group and he knew that it had worked with at least four others. Ziller had implied that the pressure on him was related to tax evasion. Better to be a crook than a pervert.

The CIA were running a full-scale surveillance on Senator Heller and it looked as if he still wasn't ready to abandon his crusade against Joe Maguire. The FBI agent who listened to the phone taps and read the surveillance reports suggested that Heller was the kind of man who would react favourably to some small friendly gesture by Maguire but Brodsky at the CIA had said there wasn't a chance of doing that.

Chapter Twenty-Nine

Josip Smit was wearing a faded denim shirt and a pair of khaki chinos. His real name wasn't Smit but the Josip was genuine. His room in the old house was small. Just space enough to take a single bed, a small cupboard and wash-bowl. The rest of his worldly goods were in a canvas hold-all on the floor between his feet.

He had a paperback copy of *The Great Gatsby* on the table beside him next to a small wire-bound notebook and a radio. The radio was a cheap local product made in Zagreb with a plastic body and a few controls. There was a switch to move it from FM through Medium-wave, Long-wave and Short-wave. There was an extra press button on the back of the case that was not marked but could split short-wave into upper or lower sideband.

Josip Smit had originally been hired to service the anti-quated hardware in the local Party office. Half a dozen golf-ball typewriters, a couple of copying machines, a fax machine and four second-generation computers. He earned the equivalent of twenty-four dollars a month but had various small privileges like being allowed to buy proper toilet rolls from the office and to have an old-age pensioners' pass although he was only just coming up to his thirtieth birthday. Although he didn't know it he was also one of the very few useful CIA agents active in the Balkans.

But somebody had noticed that the computers at Party HQ were always usable while the computers used by the signals section of the Security Police logged more down time than used time. When Josip Smit was transferred to the Security Police his pay was doubled. They noted with interest that Smit could solve all the problems they had with computer hardware but wasn't the slightest bit interested in what they were used for. That was a perfect solution so far as security was concerned.

The CIA had paid little attention to intelligence from any of the Balkan states until the old Yugoslavia was being dismembered by its ethnic groups and their historical, political and religious hatreds. Josip had only had one face-to-face meeting with his CIA controller and he had realised that until he had explained the difference the American had thought that the Balkans and the Baltic states were the same thing. But the CIA man had made clear that Josip was highly regarded for his first six months' work. They paid him in US dollars. A hundred dollars a month in cash through the embassy and another hundred dollars paid monthly into a numbered Deutsche Bank account in Berlin.

Josip Smit had a rather tangled communication set-up. Although he was a competent radio man he had never learned Morse code and was rated as being incapable of learning it, so the instructions from the CIA came via what was known in the business as 'numbers' radio. He simply had to tune in to his allotted frequency on odd number days and take down the numbers read out in English in groups of five by a man's or a woman's voice. They would be read out at five minutes past the hour every hour from twelve noon to midnight Central European time. *The Great Gatsby* provided the numbers shift for decoding.

He looked at his watch. Ten minutes to go. Carefully and meticulously Josip Smit arranged the radio and his notebook and pencil. He wondered what they would want this time. They were obviously scared that nuclear weapons could filter through from the unpaid Soviet army to Milosovic and his stooges.

He adjusted the light-weight headphones that he wore so that nobody could hear the strange broadcast that was just numbers read out slowly in a rather sexy woman's voice. He tuned in to the frequency and almost immediately he heard the bell-chimes that always preceded the broadcast. But the text was distorted, going from loud to just the hiss of white sound before it resumed. He had thought of trying to fit an automatic gain control but decided against it. If he was picked up and they found modifications to the radio it would be cited as an offence. He couldn't risk using, or even possessing, a radio that wasn't the standard government model for 'the people'. The first broadcast was hopeless and he listened over the next two hours and was able to cobble together enough to make some sense out of their message.

Even after he had melded the recognisable material from the three broadcasts the message was barely understandable.

The Americans wanted details and the Zagreb address of the HQ of the security police and the map coordinates of the oil-fields at Karlovac. They obviously didn't realise that those oil-fields hadn't been operative since the Albanians had bombed the place with two rickety old fighter-bombers borrowed from their friends in Belgrade. And that had been a year ago when nobody had worked out finally who was on whose side. He could have told them that it would end up as Serbs versus the rest. With a little help of course from over what used to be the border between Yugoslavia and Romania. He wondered why the Americans didn't realise that there never had been maps with co-ordinates because no official body had ever existed to do such work. And these days having even a school atlas could land you in jail.

He wrote them a report on the difficulties of reception especially in sun-spot conditions. The signals sergeant from the US Embassy would pick it up in its plastic bag in the cistern at the toilets at the tatty disco on Tkalciceva Street. The sergeant coded the message and transmitted it in Morse to Langley. Josip guessed the arrangement wouldn't run long because the guy who ran the disco was a Serb, and the bouncer always flashed around an AK47 after 9 p.m.

There were a lot of Josip Smits dotted around the map of central Europe and on the borders of Soviet Russia. They were not James Bonds, they wouldn't know a Magnum from a PPK and they didn't have glamorous girl-friends unless they were particularly handsome. They worked in low-grade jobs in consulates, party offices and government agencies as filing clerks, cleaners, messengers and general dogs-bodies. Their only technical skill was operating copying machines. A lot of what they passed on to their CIA controllers was dross, but from time to time there was information of real value. The problem had always been communication. Numbers radio was fine, but reception over long distances by short-wave was unreliable and sometimes confusing. The CIA, SIS in London, the BND in Germany and Mossad in Israel all found it necessary to put up with the problems of reception but were constantly working to improve their 'numbers' radio operations.

The British and the Americans tended to work well together because they both had large establishments monitoring the world's radio and telephone transmissions. GCHQ in Cheltenham and the NSA in Fort George Meade.

But all that sophistication couldn't solve the problem of transmitting over long distances with signal strengths that were suitable for reception by ordinary domestic radios. It was always the last item on the agendas of their joint meetings. It was discussed on the basis of technical reports which virtually suggested that the only solution so far as the CIA was concerned was to move Zagreb, Vilnius and Prague a couple of hundred miles west to be nearer the United States.

It was at the June CIA-NSA joint meeting that several problems seemed to have been solved at the same time. It was Brodsky who put the question.

'What if we could move the transmitter site nearer the target areas?'

Cooper from the National Security Agency, the US monitoring facility, smiled, 'It's just a problem of security. We'd need to stick a piece of the United States into somewhere in Europe.'

'So what's the problem? We could buy or rent a base for our operations.'

'That's not enough. Most of what we do would be classed as illegal in another country. We need to have an installation that is virtually the USA.'

Brodsky said quietly, 'We've got such a place already.'

'Where?'

'We've got a piece of a big sprawling complex in the UK that we share with the Royal Air Force and where our part is deemed to be US territory so far as UK laws are concerned.'

'What's it used for and where is it?'

'It's in East Anglia. It's called Mildenhall, an airfield and it's a joint RAF/USAF operation covering deep reconnaissance and counter-attack measures. The two airforces are independent of one another but on the same site and there is a large element of joint operation.'

'Is the US element independent?'

'Yeah. We police all our area and we are responsible for its maintenance.'

'Could the Brits walk in if they wanted to?'

'I guess if there was a serious crime like murder they'd want to be involved.'

Cooper said, 'Who'd bear the costs? Our budget is far too tight for us to take it on.'

Brodsky said, 'CIA would take it over. We're already using part of the site we took over for special CIA operations.'

Cooper shrugged. 'Can we go over and take a look at it?'

'Sure. I can arrange that. Next week OK for you?'

'Yes. If it's a US air force base can we fly there direct?'

'No problem.'

They had spent three days at the site and because the Mildenhall base was being slowly run down by the UK as a post cold-war economy there were several suitable sites. A draft agreement was drawn up and somebody in Whitehall had given it his seal of approval. The buildings on their part of the site were empty and in good order. From the 20th July the complex was designated as Site 390 and was technically under the control of the senior USAF officer, a general, joint commander of what was officially RAF/USAF Mildenhall in the county of Suffolk. In fact, the radio facility was an appendix to the MK Ultra operation.

Brodsky had already met the signals people who would run the numbers radio operation when he was in the USA. They were technician sergeants but they would be in civilian attire while at Mildenhall. They were obviously technically competent and they had been operating the system in the USA. There were two senior signals intelligence officers in charge of the actual radio traffic and a young woman who would be doing some of the 'numbers' readings.

For the first night's transmissions they were aiming to

contact the three most difficult agent locations. One in Warsaw, one in Belorus and the third was Josip Smit in Zagreb.

That night Josip was anxious to deal with the earliest transmission so that he could take his new girl-friend, Magda, to the cinema to see the old black-and-white classic *The Battleship Potemkin*. He had managed to obtain a bowl of hot water from the old *babcha* who supervised the building and he sat on the bed with his feet in the warm water as he arranged the bits and pieces for his radio rituals.

When he put on the headphones and plugged them into the radio he wondered if he had mistuned it. There was none of the usual slush that always preceded the numbers. Then, suddenly, there were the bells that heralded his transmissions. A brief silence and then the numbers. Slowly and clearly. He could hardly believe his ears as he wrote down the groups. Forty-two groups of five numbers. And then the single bell sign-off. As he switched off the radio he could hardly believe it. It was 7s or even 8s and so clear. He checked the radio but everything was as usual. Maybe it was the weather. Sun-spots maybe. Whatever it was it wasn't likely to be permanent. It took him an hour with the paperback to decode the message. The first item was a request for him to report on reception as soon as possible. Secondly, they wanted to know what the local population felt about the Serbs. Just as a check he tuned in to the local radio station and its signal was just normal strength.

He dried his feet, put on a clean shirt and looked out of the small dust-encrusted window. It was raining again so he would have to wear his best shoes. Bata with rubber soles.

Magda hadn't been impressed by *The Battleship Potemkin* but she'd let him take her to the cemetery on the way back to her place. The tourist office claimed that the cemetery at Mirogoj was the most beautiful in Europe. It was now mainly a night-time meeting-place for homeless lovers. But it was well cared-for and people said that the inmates were better looked after than they would have been if they were still alive.

He was back before the last of his transmissions and it was just as strong a signal as the first time. Maybe things were going to change. Maybe it was safe to ask them for more money. He heard machine-gun shots from some-where across the square and then answering fire from an AK47 and the dull thud of grenades. It was going to be one of those nights.

Chapter Thirty

There were a dozen or so people assembled in the conference room. All of them CIA or NSA and as Charlie Brodsky looked around he realised that it was appallingly bad security. One hand-grenade would have virtually wiped out the top people in CIA Special Operations. But they'd got to get on with it and Brodsky nodded to the man sitting next to him who took off his jacket and hung it carefully on the back of his chair before he started speaking.

'Gentlemen. First my apologies for asking you to come so far out of town for what is likely to be quite a short meeting. But it is important that every one of you knows how important this thing is.' He paused and looked around the table. 'If I say that it's as important and vital to our security as the secrets of the Atom bomb, I wouldn't be exaggerating.' He smiled and looked around the table again. 'And who the hell am I you might ask. My name's Hague. Morton Hague. And I hold the professorship of cryptographic mathematics at MIT.' He paused. 'I'm not CIA but I have a permanent consultancy agreement with the Agency, and with the National Security Agency.' He shrugged. 'Let me pass you back to someone you know well – Charlie Brodsky, Chief of Special Operations.'

Hague leaned back in his chair and nodded to Brodsky.

'I just want to explain briefly what this operation is all about. There'll be questions you'll want to ask me or the professor when we've both finished and most of your questions we won't answer for security reasons. So bear that in mind.

'There are parts of the world, parts of Europe even, that are virtually unknown so far as we are concerned. Latvia, Lithuania are among them but recently we've had to turn our attention to the Balkans. The Slav communities. Bosnia, Serbia, Croatia, Armenia and what had originally been Yugoslavia. We not only had no local connections but we had the problem of language. I did a check of language qualifications of all our CIA people in Europe. Not one spoke a foreign language fluently.' He sighed. 'I am told that it is CIA policy not to use people who can speak the local language in case they succumb to the blandishments of the locals.' He paused. 'Our colleagues at the National Security Agency are not interested in employing any staff who are not competent in another language. They have thousands of linguists who can not only speak all the world languages but can translate coded messages in Gaelic and Swahili or Kikuyu for example.

'So,' he sighed. 'We have to devise, with the help of NSA, a simple means of contacting our rather shaky network of agents in the Balkans. I don't need to explain it but it's called the "numbers" system.

'Our apprentice agent in one of these countries has, in

the past few days, passed us some information that could put the CIA and even more importantly the NSA into a dominating position in the whole field of communication intelligence. Our agent has no idea of the value of what he passed to us, neither does the CIA agent who acts as his go-between from the US embassy.

'So what's the problem? The problem is that we have 90% of a formula but it's useless without the last 10%. That's what this operation's about. Getting hold of that 10% is vital. Vital to the CIA and the NSA and vital to the security of the US of A.' He paused. 'Leave any questions you've got until the Prof. has done his bit.' He looked at Hague. 'It's all yours.'

'I'm sure you've all heard of the Enigma decoding machine that the Brits used during World War 2. Before the Enigma it could take a month or more of top-grade computing to break that day's code. By that time the information was useless. With the benefit of Enigma the Brit commanders were able to read the signals of all German coded radio at the same time as their German recipients. Navy, Army and the Luftwaffe. There are some who say that it was Enigma that won the war.

'What we're talking about here is cryptography, and with our resources we can break any code fairly quickly. However ...' and he took a deep breath '... we now have the problem of quantum cryptography. It is so complex that I couldn't explain it even to a high-grade mathematician. And if one of you said he could understand my explanation we'd have him at the university tonight.' He smiled. 'Probably chained up.

'So again – what's the problem? Both individuals,

commercial organisations and intelligence organisations cannot live with others who can communicate in an unbreakable code and certain people, mainly amateurs, devised a scheme called "public key" systems. They work on the principle of a safe with two keys, one to lock the safe which can be public but there's only a private key that will open the safe. So everyone can have a key to lock the safe but only one person has the key that will open it again. It is mathematically possible to compute the private key from the figures of the public key.' He paused. 'There is, at the moment, only one snag. It is reliably estimated that to do so would occupy the full-time use of the most up-to-date computer for 12 billion years. Take it from me that improving on this time will be for the next millennium if ever.

'What our man overseas gave us was the bulk of their own formula for encrypting top-secret messages. With that last 10% we are unstoppable. Thank you for listening.'

Brodsky looked around. 'Any questions?'

'What country is involved?'

'Forget it. The guy with glasses'

'Why are CIA involved when the beneficiary is obviously the NSA and its monitoring program?'

'Because NSA doesn't have the remit or the resources to do it for themselves.' He paused. 'You ma'am.'

'What chance of success do we have?'

Brodsky was obviously considering a reply and then he shook his head. 'Forget it. OK. That's enough. Don't try and chat up the Prof. or me. Take care.'

*

Brodsky had arranged for one of NSA's computer gurus to be given a temporary posting to the embassy in Zagreb. Neither the embassy nor State had been asked for their agreement and Carl Logan had settled down to conditions of maximum inconvenience. No office, no telephone, no free meals in the embassy café. When they realised that Logan was not CIA but NSA and back home could listen to all their telephone conversations both in and out of the embassy, things improved.

In the sole of his Reeboks was the folded photocopy of Public Key 1 wrapped in a plastic envelope. He looked at it from time to time to make himself feel wanted. His CIA colleague was neither numerate nor particularly literate but they rubbed along together without any great tension.

In the brief talk he'd had with Professor Hague, the Professor had said that there would be no definitive way of recognising the value of what he was shown. If it mentioned or used polynomial algorithms for prime-factorisation and discrete logarithms on a quantum computer, that would be good enough. If it looked like rubbish then still accept it but make no comment. The local CIA man wouldn't recognise Pythagoras let alone P.W. Shor's textbook. The Prof. had said that if this thing was a success he would be offered a place at a new organisation called The Centre for Quantum Computation based at the University of Oxford.

Chapter Thirty-One

Because it involved a foreign and 'unfriendly' country and had a lot of unknown hazards it wasn't going to be the usual Karla set-up, just him and the girl. Langley insisted on a trained CIA man being in charge of the logistics and there had to be the man from NSA who would be able to recognise that what was being handed over was what they wanted. Kelly from the CIA had gone to Zagreb a week before the intended meeting with Josip Smit and had booked Fulton and the girl into the Central Hotel opposite the train station on Branimirova. Two adjoining single rooms both in false names and backed up with forged passports and documentation. Zagreb was full of United Nations personnel with fat expense allowances and hotels had to be booked well ahead. Only by using the US Embassy clout was Kelly able to make the formal booking.

Kelly and Logan, the NSA man, would both stay at the embassy. When the transfer had been made Kelly would handle the pay-off. Fulton and the girl would take a taxi to the airport at Pleso. From Zagreb they would fly to Budapest and wait for instructions from his controller at Langley. Neither of them, Kelly nor Logan, had ever met the girl but they had coffee with Fulton while he explained what was planned. When Kelly raised the subject of a pistol, Fulton insisted that only the girl would be armed and then if something went wrong and she was caught the other side would never be able to untangle who she was. But he'd shown her a photo of Josip Smit.

There was only one problem outstanding and that was when to transfer her from Rosie to Karla. He wanted to wait until the last minute because his great fear was that Karla could get out of control. Four hours was the longest he'd had to cope with so far but that was when the operation was more precisely choreographed. Josip Smit had insisted that they met in the cemetery and Fulton wondered what her reaction would be in the dark, in a strange place, surrounded by gravestones and tombs and none of it properly rehearsed. And only the NSA man would have a torch so that he could check Smit's documents.

They had chosen that night because there was an important football match, Croatia Zagreb versus some team from Bosnia, and the streets would be busy and the police well-occupied.

They left both hire cars in separate places on the periphery of the cemetery with the car that Fulton and the girl would use parked near the cemetery's main gates. Gates that were never closed.

There had been no problem transferring the girl from Rosie to Karla but she seemed on edge as he drove her to the cemetery. They were in good time and they had found the tomb with the name Strossmayer just visible in the mossy stonework. They crouched down beside the tomb and then they heard voices.

When the shadowy figures of the CIA man and the NSA man became visible Fulton touched the girl's arm. 'Let's go slowly.' And then, to his horror he saw her pull out the pistol. 'Put that away, Karla. Put it away.' And then he saw the figure of Smit about ten feet away from them, the sudden flash of the NSA man's torch and as Smit reached inside his jacket for the papers she fired the gun at the three of them. Again and again. He rushed to where they lay. Smit was dead already, the papers still in his hand. Fulton took them without looking at them and moved to the two Americans. The NSA man was dead and Kelly was unconscious and covered in blood. Fulton was panic-stricken and hurried the girl back to their car and headed for the station, changed his mind and followed a sign that said Aeroport Pleso 17 km.

Half-way to the airport he turned into the open gates of a farm, switched off the engine and turned to look at the girl. She looked quite calm and he breathed a sigh of relief as he talked her slowly back to Rosie, taking the gun from her hand as he talked. He took a deep breath as he looked at her but realised that it would be pointless to ask her why she had shot them. She wouldn't know what he was talking about. Thank God all their kit was in the boot of the car. He'd get them on the first plane no matter where it was going.

He backed the car onto the road and headed in the direction of the airport. There was plenty of room in the airport car-park and Fulton carried their bags into the terminal hall. The timetable above the counter had only one place that he recognised. Rome. They could be there in a couple of hours, book in a hotel and he could think what he should do.

The sales-girl told him that seats had to be booked in advance and he did what one automatically had to do in such countries. He slid a hundred dollars across the counter with his book of travellers cheques. He got a smile and two business-class seats. The flight would be called in an hour and he kept one holdall and checked in the rest of their luggage and walked her to the late-night café. There were no seats, just a counter with several self-help machines for tea, coffee and juices. They both opted for coffee which wasn't too bad but there was no sugar.

She was talking about the green stains on her light-coloured skirt and wondering where they had come from but she was delighted when he told her that they were going to stay in Rome for a few days. She had never been to Italy.

When they took off the plane was half-empty and the elderly attendant told them that only fruit juices were available on Avioimpex flights to Rome which was considered to be only a short-haul destination from Zagreb. There had been no passport or security check.

The girl had slept as soon as they took off and Fulton was alone with his thoughts. His incredible nightmare thoughts. He went back over the events in the cemetery. She must have thought that when Josip Smit put his hand inside his jacket that he was reaching for a gun. That was what she had been taught to think when she was being trained at Langley. And in the league she operated in, when a man reached for a gun, you shot him. When Kelly screamed at her she couldn't make out what he was saying but his anger was all too obvious. Fulton had told her that there would be no guns but the CIA man had pulled out a gun and she'd seen it shine in the streetlight before she fired at him.

Fulton could hardly bring himself to think of the outcome. Josip Smit, a valuable agent, was dead, a computer expert from NSA was dead. And by now Fulton was pretty sure that Kelly was dead too. The only hope was that the papers he had taken off Smit's body were what the bastards wanted.

In the aircraft toilet Fulton slid the bolt on the door and put his foot against the bottom of the door. There were not as many papers as he had expected. Most of it was wrapping-paper to protect the four sheets of computer paper. But they had not been used in a computer. They ran the length of the pages and were solely long mathematical formulas crowded with Greek letters and maths signs that he had never seen before. He had no idea whether this was what Brodsky and the others wanted so desperately. As Fulton folded the papers carefully he slid them into the inside pocket of his jacket. Then he reached for the canvas bag between his feet, stood up and let the gun slide quietly into the toilet hoping to God that the flushing system would work. It did.

As Fulton leaned back in his seat he knew that he was kidding himself. If those papers in his pocket were what they wanted, they were his only chance of coming out of this débâcle alive. He looked at his watch. It was just after midnight but it all seemed to have been long ago. By now they'd probably have heard about the death of Kelly and the NSA man. Nobody at the embassy would know anything of Josip Smith and the rest of it.

Chapter Thirty-Two

Brodsky cursed as he reached for the phone on his bedside table and looked at his watch. 5 a.m.

'Yeah. What is it?'

'There's a call from Zagreb for you personally, sir.'

'Who from?'

'His Excellency, sir. Our ambassador.'

'What's his name?'

'Niel Lundgren, sir.'

'Put him through.'

The call came straight through.

'Is that Mr Brodsky?'

'It is, ambassador. What can I do for you?'

'You could start by sending somebody over to take charge of two dead bodies. Both American citizens. I'm told that they both work for your outfit. I'd like to see the back of them.'

Brodsky was silent for long moments and then he said, 'What are their names, these dead men?'

'Just clear them out. I've been called to the Croats'

251

Foreign Secretary to give an explanation about two dead Americans and one dead Croat. I've never wanted your people inside the embassy. You're just trouble-makers wherever you go. And when you run out of road you expect us, the diplomats you people sneer at, to get you out of the crap.'

'And who suggested that you phone me?'

'I looked in the files of one of them – he was your chap here in the embassy – name of Kelly.'

'Is he one of the casualties?'

'He's dead. Shot in the head.'

'What happened?'

'How the hell should I know. So far as I can tell there were only three people there. Two Americans and one Croat. And they're all dead. All shot in the head.'

'Where did this happen?'

'In a bloody cemetery for God's sake.'

Brodsky sighed and turned to sit on the edge of the bed.

'Right. Where are the bodies of the two Americans?'

'In the city morgue.'

'OK. Leave things as they are. Say nothing to the locals and say nothing, repeat nothing, to the media. I'll be at the embassy this evening.'

'I shan't be here. I'm attending a dinner given by the Chinese legation.'

Brodsky held back the expletive and said, 'Have a wonderful evening mister ambassador.'

At the embassy His Excellency was seething. He had had a personal call from the Secretary of State to do whatever

Brodsky wanted done to get the bodies released. To fuel his anger the Secretary of State spoke as if it was all his fault. It was hinted that his expected promotion to Athens was dependent on his efficient cooperation.

Brodsky's assistant had gathered up the belongings and files of the two Americans and Brodsky himself had identified the two corpses at the mortuary.

His assistant had checked at the hotel for Fulton and the girl but it seemed that they had both checked out, leaving their rooms empty despite having paid in advance for a week's stay. A local undertaker had been paid for the two simple coffins and there had been no mention by anyone, embassy, Croat officialdom or Brodsky, of Josip Smit. But Brodsky gathered that nobody had claimed the body.

His Excellency didn't volunteer to accompany Brodsky and his party back to the airfield. Brodsky slept most of the way on the return journey and tried not to think of what had happened to Fulton, the girl and the magic piece of paper, and all the official palaver that would have to be gone through back in Washington.

The man in the blue overalls had cursed as he tried to ease out the obstruction but in the end it hung down from the outlet. The servicing crew were used to finding some pretty strange things in aircraft toilets but it was the first time the obstruction had turned out to be a pistol. It was a Smith and Wesson and he wrapped it loosely and carefully in a toilet tissue and took it across to the police guard-room. The police called the Security Police who weren't interested but arrived half an hour later.

The next day back in Zagreb a police arms specialist gave them his report. There was one bullet left in the chamber and it looked as if five bullets had been discharged. Almost as an after-thought, he suggested that somebody from forensics should check the weapon for fingerprints.

The prints turned out to be virtually useless without special treatment but the expert suggested that the weapon had been used by a woman because there was evidence of moisturising cream and a fleck of nail-varnish near the safety catch.

A week of plodding police-work ended with the authorities claiming that the gun was the weapon that had killed the two Americans and the Croat in the cemetery. A process of elimination pointed to a Miss Joan Piper, an American citizen. Last seen on flight 904 from Zagreb to Cairo with a stop in Rome.

It was confirmed that it was the US Embassy in Zagreb which had made the booking at the Central Hotel for two Americans in adjoining single rooms in the names of Peter Cramer and Miss Joan Piper. They had not returned to their rooms on the night of the murder but a hire-car in the name of Cramer had been left at the airport and two seats had been booked on the flight to Rome. When the rooms had been booked at the Central Hotel, the embassy official concerned had claimed that both the man and the woman were temporary embassy staff.

A search of Josip Smit's small room had revealed nothing of police interest and the office he worked for at the Security Police HQ said that Smit was both efficient and not involved in the organisation's work. After a grainy picture of Smit had appeared in the local paper, it had been recognised by his girl-friend but although she had said nothing to anyone, official or otherwise, she was a nice sentimental girl and had put a small bunch of daisies on the top of the tomb that they had enjoyed from time to time in the past year.

More to annoy the US embassy people than in expectation of any cooperation, the Zagreb police asked them for details of the two Americans at the hotel.

When they received no reply they sent a summons from the Prosecutor General's office claiming that an order of extradition might be issued as the Americans were suspected of being involved in a crime of violence. It was at that point that Charlie Brodsky became involved again.

When, on the same day, he received a phone call from Fulton, he was not in the best of humour.

'Where the hell are you?'

'I've been phoning you for several days but there's been no response.'

Brodsky noticed the evasion. 'Where are you?'

'In Rome.'

'What the hell are you doing there?'

'Just keeping out of the way.'

'Who's way — mine or the bloody Croats?'

'Let me tell you what happened.'

'No way, my friend, not on a public telephone-line. You get right back where I can meet you. Is the girl with you still?'

'Yes.'

'Don't come back to the US.'

'Why not?'

'There's two applications for you and her to be returned to Zagreb as suspects in a crime of violence.' He paused. 'Go back to that dump in the UK. Both of you. I'll contact you in a couple of days.' And Brodsky slammed down the receiver. Fulton hesitated and then called Brodsky again.

'Brodsky.'

'You've got to remember that the girl has no idea of what happened.'

By the time that he was heading from Tunbridge Wells to Tenterden, Brodsky had calmed down. What was important now was sweeping it all under the carpet.

At the cottage he had been polite and amiable to the girl but as he looked at her, a pretty young woman, he realised that she was the real problem. Fulton could be side-tracked easily enough, but the girl was a walking pantechnicon of some of the most ruthless actions taken for the CIA that could bring down not just MK Ultra but the whole of the CIA. She looked like any pretty secretary at Langley but in reality she was a potential disaster.

Fulton had booked a room for Brodsky at a local hotel and they used booking him in as an excuse to get away from the girl and the cottage.

When Brodsky had settled in he pointed to one of the other armchairs.

'Tell me what happened.'

Brodsky listened carefully without interrupting until

he realised that maybe Fulton still had the missing section of the code-breaking formula.

'You say you took the papers before you left the cemetery?'

'Yeah.'

'Where are they now?'

'In a safe place.'

'Don't try and play games with me, Fulton, or your feet won't touch. What is it you want?'

'A new identity and a safe source of income.'

'You'll get that anyway. You don't imagine we want you wandering around as a target for every lunatic who thinks knocking you off is an easy way to earn a buck.'

'Do I have your word for that?'

'You've got it. You're wasting time.'

'Tell me the deal.'

'The deal I had in mind was a hundred grand free of tax and a tax-free annual pension of the same amount. And we'll discuss with you where you want to live and your security and documentation.'

Fulton nodded and leaned forward untying his shoe-laces, taking off his right shoe and easing out the flattened paper which he handed to Brodsky without looking at it.

Brodsky reached for his brief-case and slid the papers inside. As he turned back to Fulton Brodsky said, 'What have you got in mind for the girl? Is she a hundred per cent safe?'

Fulton shrugged. 'There's no such thing when hypnotism has been involved.'

'Well, I'm going to leave that problem for you to solve.

You're the expert but make sure there's no loopholes. She's a loose cannon and don't forget it.'

'When can we finalise my deal?'

'Deal with the girl and then contact me. It can be done in a couple of days.'

Chapter Thirty-Three

The flat landscape of the Romney Marshes looked burnished by the sinking sun. It was 10 p.m. and warm for the time of year. Fulton tried to breathe slowly and deeply but his hands were trembling as they lay in his lap. For a few moments he sat with his eyes closed and then, desperate to get it over, he said, 'Are you OK, Karla?'

She shrugged. 'I'm OK. Where are we going?'

'There's something special I want to tell you about.' He paused. 'Some time soon I'm going to release you and when I say the words I want you to walk towards the water. Any water. A lake, the sea, or maybe a river. And when I say those words I want you to walk to the water and when your feet are wet you go on walking until you've counted slowly up to two hundred.'

'And then what?'

'Then you'll be Rosie and Joanna again.'

He started the engine and turned off the main road and across the bridge to where the road sign was barely visible. It said 'Camber Sands 2 miles'.

Five minutes later he stopped the car and got out, reaching inside to help the girl across the front seats.

As she stood beside him smoothing down her skirt, he could see the last light on the sea.

He turned to look at her. 'When I say – Karla, there's always tomorrow – I want you to do what I told you to do. D'you understand?'

She shrugged. 'Whatever you say.'

He walked with her to the sea-wall and then said slowly and clearly, 'Karla. There's always tomorrow. Do it.'

He was aware of her hand going to her hair in the breeze as he hurried back to the car, turned it in the narrow road and drove off in the direction of Rye.

An hour later he had gone back to where he had left her but there was no sign of her.

Brodsky was contemplating a pre-emptive three no trumps, when the phone rang. His three companions laid their hands face down on the baize-topped card-table. He picked up the phone.

'Brodsky. Who is it?'

'It's a UK call. The operator says it is the Special Branch officer for Maidstone.'

'Where the hell is that?'

'It's the county town of Kent, sir.'

'Did he say it was urgent?'

'No. But I think it is.'

'OK. Put him on.' He paused. 'Charlie Brodsky speaking, officer. How can I help you?'

'There's been a car accident on the A21, sir. A petrol

tanker and a Ford Escort were in collision. Several casualties and one dead. The one in the Ford. We checked his clothing and wallet. That's why we decided to contact you immediately. He's an American citizen with two passports. One in the name of Peter Cramer, the other in the name of Dr J. Fulton. There is what looks like genuine ID linking him to the CIA, sir. And various notes that refer to you and some sort of financial arrangement.'

'You're quite sure he's dead?'

'Quite sure, sir. He's very dead.'

'What's your name please?'

'Inspector Holland, sir.'

'Thanks for contacting me so promptly. You did the right thing. I'll get my people to contact you in the next hour or so. Bye.'

He put the receiver back slowly onto the cradle and looked around at his companions.

'I'm sorry. I gotta go. Just one of those things.'

As Brodsky made the various contacts he listened carefully and tried to assess whether any response or any voice indicated that they already knew what he was telling them. There were no such signs. Maybe he was losing his grip. Thank God he'd already got the documentation from Fulton.

                                        College, Sunday night

Dear Charles

I was sorry to hear of your chap's demise and I thought it might ease the wound a little if I let you know that the material that he obtained in such strange circumstances was actually what we hoped for.

However, and quantum maths is full of howevers, there is of course a new problem.

The finished version is what we'd have to call a building-block. It lacks what I'd call mathematical elegance. I would estimate that your people's efforts have saved us at least 7–8 months' work. And I suspect that at the end of it all, E will still equal MC squared.

Yours ever,

Martin.

Chapter Thirty-Four

PC Cooper leaned over the counter and asked the operator to get him the Special Branch Officer based at Lewes, the HQ of the Sussex Police.

'I'll take it in my office.'

As he walked to his small office in the police-station at Rye he checked his watch. It was a few minutes past midnight on a Sunday night.

The phone rang as he pulled out his chair and sat down.

'Hi. This is McBride. What can I do for you?'

'PC Cooper at Rye. I've got a problem. I thought you ought to know about it. I was doing a car patrol at Camber Sands and came across a young woman sitting in the dark, alone, on the sea-wall. I asked her if she was OK and she seemed to have difficulty in talking. Cutting a long story short she seemed to me to be drugged. She didn't know who she was and didn't know what she was doing there. She spoke with what could be an American accent and seemed to be under the impression that I was a CIA officer.'

'Where is she now?'

'They're giving her a snack and a coffee in the interrogation room. We're never busy on Sundays after eleven.'

'How old is she?'

'I'd guess about early or middle twenties.'

'Have you searched her?'

'No. I don't have just cause. She's not charged with anything and so far as we're concerned she's just a person in distress.'

'Has your quack seen her?'

'No.'

'Tell me what she said that made you think she thought you were CIA.'

'She just said it in so many words – like it's all right for you, you're CIA. Nothing very specific.'

'When do you go off duty?'

'I've got another four hours yet.'

'Don't let anybody else question her. I'll come over right away.' He paused. 'Contact your quack and ask him to stand by in case I need him.'

'OK. You know where we are?'

'You bet. I've got a boat down there.'

Special Branch Officer McBride tried to think of organisations whose initials were CIA but were not the United States' Central Intelligence Agency. Camber Sands where the woman had been picked up was a sprawl of holiday chalets blessed by the most beautiful sandy beach. Film companies used it to shoot scenes that were supposed to be in Africa and apart from a few small shops that was all Camber Sands consisted of. It's nearest small town, Rye, one of the ancient Cinque Ports, was where he was heading. There were drug-related problems in many of the south-coast towns but Rye was the least likely to be involved in the drug scene. Perched on a hill with a fortress wall, its life was tourists, fishing and serving the many local farms. At the best of times the police-station at Rye was not troubled by major crime and since the cut-backs there would be only two officers on duty at night. One in the office, the other on patrol.

There were two cars parked at the side of the police-station and McBride parked alongside them. He reached onto the back seat and lifted out the tape-recorder and his note-book. A police constable was waiting for him at the door. They shook hands and PC Cooper introduced himself and said, 'I've kept our telephone girl on in case we need her. The station's usually only manned by one person after 11 p.m. Let's go along to Interrogation.'

There was a half-eaten sandwich and a Thermos of coffee on the table in front of the girl who didn't turn her head as the two men walked in. McBride saw that she was very beautiful. Long dark hair, big heavy-lidded eyes, and a soft full mouth. He sat down in front of her.

'How are you feeling now?'

She shook her head slowly but said nothing and McBride carried on.

'We're a bit worried about you. Is there anything we could do to help you?'

She looked back at him and said softly, 'I've had enough. I can't go on with this any more.'

'Tell me what the problem is,' McBride said quietly. 'Is there anyone you'd like us to contact for you? Your parents maybe? Or a friend?'

She sighed and shook her head.

'I think a doctor should look you over. What do you think?'

For a moment she looked at his face and then she screamed again and again, trying to stand up, clutching at the table to keep her balance before she groaned as she fell to the floor.

McBride said, 'Is the doctor here?'

'He can be here in five minutes.'

'Get him then. Tell him it's an emergency.'

McBride took off his jacket and folded it, sliding it under the girl's head. Her face was deathly pale and she was gasping for breath.

The doctor stood washing his hands in the small toilet and McBride stood at the open door.

'What d'you think, doc?'

'You'd better call an ambulance. I'll speak to the hospital myself.' The doctor turned, wiping his hands on paper from a roll of kitchen paper. 'I'd say she's coming out of a dose of drugs. I may be wrong but I'd put my bet on some sort of hallucinogen – probably LSD.' He paused, looking at McBride. 'She had a spate of talking. None of it made sense but did you notice her accent?'

'Not particularly.'

'I'd say it was American or Canadian. Boston or somewhere like that.'

'Is she physically OK?'

'Needs feeding up a bit but otherwise OK. It's her mind that's the problem. The babble had distinct overtones of psychosis.'

'She thought the officer who found her was CIA. That fits in with the American accent.'

'Fits in with the psychosis too.'

McBride had phoned his HQ at Scotland Yard who had passed the report routinely to MI5's own HQ at Thames House. With the mention of the CIA in the report, MI5 had passed it to SIS Liaison who shuffled it to Vauxhall Bridge. The same day a memo came through that the matter should be considered as urgent if SIS were interested. Otherwise the police would have to take over the unidentified woman and some arrangements made to have her cared for. She had neither identification nor financial resources. During the second medical check it had been noticed that she had a small tattoo on the sole of her right foot. It was just the letters MK which were assumed to possibly be her initials. Hargreaves at SIS was given the job of checking out the mystery lady who seemed to think that the simple cop who found her was something to do with the CIA. And who had some sort of trauma when you suggested that a doctor should see her.

The police had suggested he booked in at the Mermaid Inn in the centre of the old town. He had brought one of SIS's consultant psychotherapists with him and they had adjoining rooms in the old inn. He had briefed the specialist on the journey down and had let him read the few memos and reports relating to the case.

The girl had been given a private room at the local hospital and Rosen, the neurologist, had been shown all the hospital records since the girl had been admitted but the admin staff were anxious to know how much longer she was expected to be at the hospital.

Rosen had spent two hours alone with the girl and it was mid-afternoon when he contacted Hargreaves again.

'You've got something pretty odd going on here, old chap.' He paused. 'It's quite serious and quite complicated. Let's go and find a coffee place.'

They had found a pleasant café in the centre of the town and they'd each ordered coffee and a cheese omelette. While they were waiting to be served, Rosen said, 'That girl's been given doses of LSD over at least a couple of years.'

'Does that mean she's an addict?'

'No. Oddly enough LSD isn't in itself addictive but you can become kind of hooked by the effects it has on you.' He shrugged. 'About as addictive as tea or coffee. But a lot more dangerous. It's a patented drug and is made only by the patentee company. A quite respectable pharmaceuticals manufacturer in Switzerland named Sandoz. But that's not the real problem in this case.'

'What is?'

'This girl has spent a large part of her recent life under hypnosis. She is still under hypnosis but I think I could normalise her given time.'

'How much time?'

'Could be a week or it could take six months. And success isn't guaranteed by any means.'

'Why would she have been hypnotised? And who would do it?'

'Who knows? But you're right, she does think the cop who picked her up is CIA. I suspect she thinks we are too.'

'What do we do with her while you're working on her?'

Rosen shrugged. 'That's up to you guys. What about one of your safe-houses?'

'Could she do us for false arrest or unauthorised detention?'

'As long as we keep a proper log and a diary I don't think any court would go against you. Especially if we can get her back in the real world and back to her old life pre-hypnosis.'

'How long could she stay under the effects of hypnosis?'

Rosen shrugged. 'Indefinitely. Until whoever hypnotised her brought her back.' He paused. 'Mind you, I'm pretty sure that this young woman is undergoing what we call "flashback". A temporary return to a hypnotic state without it necessarily being induced.'

'Did you notice the initials on the sole of her foot?'

'Yes. Strange. Unusual site. People generally indulge in tattoos to show them off. Looks like this girl was trying to hide it.' He looked at McBride. 'Do the CIA lot operate in this country?'

'We all operate in all countries. Sometimes a proper full unit, sometimes just a bod on his own. The CIA are the same. A couple of them at the embassy and the rest spread around London. They'll have some sort of liaison team at Cheltenham at GCHQ because of their close working relationship with the American outfit, NSA, their radio and telephone monitoring unit in Maryland. Big outfit. At least sixty thousand employees.' He paused. 'You go for her waffle about the CIA?'

'I don't know. 'I'd bear it in mind if I were you. She's been used under control for quite a time and her symptoms indicate that she's scared of something. Maybe scared of something she's been told to do.'

'Could you take her over yourself?'

'I could have a go but I'm not an expert on hypnosis. I'd need to have her in London and some nursing help.' He looked at his watch. 'Give London a ring, see what they want. They could decide that it's best just to let it take its course through the police and NHS channels.'

'Tell me something. Is this girl suffering from some sort of loss of memory?'

Rosen frowned. 'You're thinking of amnesia?'

'Yes.'

Rosen shrugged. 'Could be, but instinct makes me think that it's more than that.'

'Like what?'

'I think she might have been hypnotised and it's gone wrong.'

'Who could have done this?'

'I don't know. That's why I need time to find out.'

'What's in it for SIS? Why should they be involved?'

'Because she thinks every man who's talked to her is CIA and she's scared of them.' He shrugged. 'Maybe the letters CIA don't stand for Central Intelligence Agency. Maybe it's a company acronym. But if it is, why is she scared of it?'

'You think it's significant?'

'I think it's worth finding out.' He paused. 'If we can.'

SIS had gone along with Rosen's reasoning and the girl had been accommodated in a flat in Pimlico along with a retired nurse who had experience of caring for patients with mental problems. With Rosen seeing her frequently in the hope that he might be able to find out who she was and what she was doing alone in the dark at Camber Sands.

Chapter Thirty-Five

Leo Rosen was only one of several consultant psycho-therapists used from time to time by SIS. The Brits were comparative innocents so far as hypnosis and mind-control were concerned. They had developed their methods over the centuries and were satisfied that they could function successfully without indulging in what they referred to as mumbo-jumbo.

Like a good many of those who spend their time exploring the make-up of the human brain and its effects on human behaviour, Leo Rosen was aware of his own defects. In his case he had a tendency to move from observation to involvement. Especially when his patient was an attractive female. His current SIS assignment was not only physically attractive but an absorbing case in itself. How do you relate to somebody who doesn't know who they are or what their previous life had been? On her file cover she was described merely as 'Miss X'. After several months he knew no more than what the police at Rye had told him and his own analysis that she had almost certainly been hypnotised at some recent time in her life.

As time had gone by without any apparent useful result from his work with the girl, SIS had lost interest in her and suggested that his efforts should be limited to another two weeks. After that she could be handed back to the police or the social services and her fate left to them. But there was a small problem. Leo Rosen had grown fond of his lost soul. And she seemed to be fond of him too. What was worse she had obviously become dependent on him. He had gradually broken all the rules of patient-therapist relationships. With outings to restaurants and the cinema. A weekend together in a small hotel in Sussex registered as a married couple.

Rosen had a flat over his consultancy rooms off Harley Street and she had moved in with him as a receptionist ostensibly in return for a room and board.

The first time that Rosen had made a tentative pass at the girl he had been surprised. She had responded eagerly and passionately. And she was good company, amused at his jokes and looked after his day-by-day needs as if she cared about him. He had taken her around the stores to buy clothes and the things that a young woman needed and he had given her an antique gold ring with a small single diamond. There were times when Rosen wondered if it wouldn't be a good idea for them to be married.

He was shaving when he heard her scream and he rushed into the bedroom. She was sitting there with her head in her hands and when she looked up at him her face was white and she pointed at the radio.

'Stop it. Stop it. I can't do it.'

As he reached for the switch on the radio he wondered what it was all about. The radio was just playing music. Something he recognised but couldn't identify.

When the radio was off he looked back at her. She was shaking and trembling and gasping for breath. He put his arm around her shoulders and sat on the bed alongside her.

He said softly, 'Tell me what's the matter, honey.'

'I can't. They'd kill me.'

'Who would kill you?'

'Karla's people. I don't want to be Karla any more.' She sighed. 'That music on the radio. They must know.'

'What music was it?'

'From the film you showed me. The video.'

'I've never shown you a film, honey, nor a video. Tell me what it was.'

'I don't remember. Just the song.'

'Who is Karla?'

She looked shocked. 'You know who Karla is. You made me Karla.'

Rosen plumped up the pillows for her.

'Lie back, honey, and I'll get you an aspirin.'

She lay back submissively and he went downstairs and found a mild amphetamine pill. Then a thought struck him. He needed to find out what that music was. He rang Broadcasting House and was put through to Radio 2's production unit. They were helpful and came back in a few minutes. The music had been an orchestral arrangement of Lara's Song from the film *Dr Zhivago*, 'Somewhere my Love'.

As Rosen walked slowly back upstairs he guessed that the scene had been something to do with her former life. But he couldn't imagine how a piece of music had brought it all back. She was asleep when he got back to their bedroom, her face flushed now and her breathing heavy. He sat with her, holding her hand until it was time for his next appointment.

It was a case of claustrophobia and at this the first interview he explained the possible relief the patient could get from hypnosis to find what the root cause of her phobia was. His receptionist made an appointment for the following week. But Rosen's mind was with that sad figure on the bed upstairs. And he knew that he only had two choices. He could do nothing except give her sedatives and hope that whatever caused the outburst didn't happen again. Or he could try using hypnotism to see what lay behind her fears. Another odd thing was that when she'd been on about Karla her accent was definitely American.

At lunch-time he went back up to the flat to see her and she was sitting at the dressing-table brushing her long black hair. She turned to look at him, smiling, as she handed him the brush.

'How do you feel now?'

She looked surprised. 'I'm fine.'

He took her out for lunch to a small Italian restaurant that they often used and she obviously enjoyed the amiable flirting of the *padrone*.

As they walked back to the flat he knew that he didn't have the courage at that moment to try any hypnosis.

It was in the middle of the night when he woke to her screams and he switched on the bedside lamp. She was standing by the bed, her face contorted, her hand pointing at him.

'You promised. You promised I needn't be Karla again. Why . . .'

He stood up and put his arms around her. 'You aren't Karla. That's all over. Sit down by me here on the bed.'

As she sat he said softly, 'Tell me about Karla.'

'You're the one who made me into Karla. You're Fulton. I work for you.'

'Where do you work for Fulton?'

'At the CIA.'

'Where?'

'At Langley and the new place. The airfield.' She shivered. 'You made me kill those men.'

'Listen to me carefully. You are not Karla. Karla doesn't exist. You've been hypnotised. You are not Karla. You are not Karla. You are not in America and I am not the CIA. Do you understand?'

She nodded slowly and he went on. 'When I tell you to wake up you will forget all about Karla.'

She sighed. 'But you made them play the sign music. The music that makes me Karla.'

'What music?'

'The music on the radio – *Zhivago*.'

'That music doesn't make you Karla. Nothing will

ever make you Karla again. When I wake you up you'll tell me your real name.' He paused. 'Wake up nice and slowly. Nice and slowly. Open your eyes now and tell me your name.'

She opened her eyes and looked at him. 'Hi. I'm Rosie.' She smiled. 'But you know that don't you?'

'How do you feel?'

She shrugged. 'I'm fine.'

'What were we talking about?'

'I don't remember. We were just chatting about having a dog or a cat.' She laughed. 'You said better a bird in a cage.'

It was a chat they'd had a week before. He changed the subject and he spent the evening with her showing her the basic rules for playing backgammon.

As he lay awake that night beside her, he felt utterly confused. He seemed to have made things worse rather than better. Maybe he had expunged this Karla figure. But who were the mythical men she thought she had killed? And who the hell was Fulton who worked at the CIA HQ at Langley? Maybe Hargreaves at SIS could give him a lead on that. But it would mean revealing his relationship with the girl. Maybe he could work out some way of making it seem a casual enquiry and not related to the girl. He tried to find his notes covering his original sessions with the girl but they seemed to have been handed over to SIS when they took over the girl. But one thing still stuck in his mind. He seemed to remember thinking that she had been left in a hypnotic state that was more complex than simple hypnosis.

But as the days went by without any further dramas Rosen, who was a thinker rather than an investigator, decided that the trauma had been dealt with as well as was possible with so many unknown factors involved.

Chapter Thirty-Six

There were sharp gusts of wind coming off the river and shaking the canvas hood over the wheelhouse and as Maguire checked all the press-buttons he saw her talking to one of the CIA men outside the chandlery. She saw him looking and waved to him, smiling.

As she eventually stepped on board she was laughing as he took her hand to steady her. 'Greater love hath no man than this . . .'

'Than what?'

'Than letting a lady come on board in high heels.'

He laughed and guided her to the foam-filled cushions of the double seat.

'What do you fancy?'

'A gin and tonic with three ice cubes.'

As he handed her her drink and sat down opposite her, she said, 'I've left a cardboard box at the chandlery for you. They'll bring it over later.'

'What's in the cardboard box, my dear?'

'Six tea-towels – your present ones stink. New china

mugs that aren't all chipped round the tops. Six cork coasters . . .' she paused '. . . and a partridge in a pear tree.' She paused and looked at him. 'How are you? You look tired.'

He shrugged. 'I think you're right. I need a change.'

'You need a rest and *then* a change.'

'What kind of change?'

'You need to get away from the CIA and that whole world of deceit. You've done your stint, now let somebody else take over.'

He smiled indulgently at her. It was her constant theme. 'Who've you got in mind?'

'Charlie Brodsky's been working alongside you for long enough to make his own mistakes. There must be others too. But I suspect there won't be many volunteers.'

'Why not?'

'Because they know that what you do for them means you're onto a beating to nothing.'

'Tell me more.'

'Which do you prefer – the CIA or the army?'

'The army. That's what I am.'

'Because the army's honest. They make mistakes but that's because the politicians interfere with military decisions. Men who've never held a gun in their lives tell senior soldiers about when they can fire back at the people who are firing at them. They call it "the rules of engagement".' She paused. 'It's the CIA who need you. You're a cloak for what they get up to. It must be OK because Joe Maguire didn't stop us.'

For long moments Maguire was silent as he looked at her.

'You've obviously thought a lot about this. Why bother?'

'Because it angers me seeing someone I care about being abused, deliberately and indiscriminately.' She paused. 'Joe. You're right. You're a soldier, not a criminal.'

'Has Adam ever talked to you about all this?'

She shook her head. 'No. I tried to get him to talk but he refused. Said it was your life, not ours.' She sighed. 'Why don't you speak to him?'

He shrugged. 'Maybe I will.' He smiled as he looked at her calm, beautiful face. 'Thanks for thinking about me. It's a great comfort.' He sighed. 'And it gets me back in the real world again.'

'What's the real world in your estimation?'

'A world where it's normal and natural to care about other people.'

It was nearly two weeks later when Adam Kennedy mentioned to Angela that he'd talked with Joe Maguire at Joe's prompting.

'What did you tell him?'

'Nothing that he didn't know already. He's turned a blind eye to most of the games that the CIA get up to but Joe's no fool.'

'What's that mean?'

'You know sometimes in a film cartoon the little guy walks to the edge of a deep canyon and instead of stopping he goes on walking. When he's half-way across he looks down and sees the canyon below him and he falls. Right at this moment that's Joe Maguire.'

'Tell me more.'

Kennedy drew up a chair and reached to the nearby trolley and poured them both a glass of red wine. He held up his glass and said, '*Salute!*'

She smiled and said, '*A la vostra.*'

'Tell me what your feelings are for Joe Maguire.'

She shrugged and smiled. 'In my own peculiar way, I love him.'

'A father figure?'

'No way.' She laughed. 'More as a child who I want to protect.'

'Not bad, honey. Not bad.' He paused. 'When you look at Joe you have to bear something in mind. He was about thirty or thirty-five when he left the army and he's still thirty or thirty-five because he didn't really leave. He's still a soldier and you have to remember that in the army you are part of a well-tried structure. You know the rules, military and otherwise. If you become an officer you have a pattern of behaviour and responsibility laid out for you.

'From the outside the CIA looks much the same. But it ain't. It has no respect for any laws, civil or criminal. It claims that it breaks the law in a just cause – saving the US of A. And that's what Joe would go along with. But this is not an infantry patrol to take a couple of hills, it's more likely protecting people whose idea of winning is gang-raping a young woman in front of her husband. The CIA have no code of honour, nothing so filthy that they wouldn't do it or use it.

'So you have to ask yourself. Are they justified in fighting dirty against an equally dirty enemy? But remember – you can't cherry-pick. If you're prepared to torture a man to make him tell you what you want to know, you've got to take the gang-rape too. No second thoughts.

'If you want to know how long and how painful a milligram of some drug takes to kill a man, you can be a good sport and try it on a Mexican, or a Colombian. You're God. Or at least you're Gyges with his ring of invisibility.'

She shook her head. 'You'll never convince me that Joe Maguire is like that.'

'Of course he isn't. He wouldn't be any use to them if he was. Neither is Swenson for that matter who got him into that job. They're two very fine soldiers who saw the establishment turn on their troops because of Korea and Vietnam. Joe Maguire has never forgotten all that but he's got a slow-burning fuse, has Joe. It won't burn out until he's in the ground in Arlington.' He paused. 'Unless somebody shows him another way to save the country from disaster.'

'Is there such a way?'

For a moment Kennedy sat there in silence and then he eased himself slowly out of his chair and walked towards the window. For what seemed a long time he just stood there watching as the rain streamed down the window. Then he turned and looked at his sister-in-law.

'Do you really want to go on along this road?'

'Yes.'

'OK. What do you think that Joe thinks about you? Apart from the fact that you're very beautiful.'

She sighed and was silent for a few minutes before she said, 'I think he's fond of me. He's kind and sympathetic and a gentle man. I don't ever see him with other people so maybe he's like that with everybody.' She shrugged slowly. 'He always seems glad to see me and when I'm with him he doesn't really relax until he's fixed to see me again, the next time.'

Kennedy smiled. 'And like you, he's a very modest person.' He paused. 'He talks about you a lot. He obviously takes notice of anything you say and several times he's asked me outright what he could do to please you.'

She laughed softly. 'And what did you tell him?'

'Just to go on being himself. You're a pair in many ways despite the age difference. You need a rock and he needs a rainbow.'

She looked at him with obvious affection.

'Solomon in all his glory.' Smiling, she said, 'Thanks for caring.'

Chapter Thirty-Seven

———————◆———————

Joe Maguire often had a snack at the bagel bakery on Connecticut Avenue. For him it was neutral territory, a mental oasis. When he had a problem it often seemed to get solved as he sat with a toasted bagel, raisins and a cup of tea. Not that he thought about the particular problem while he was eating. He just seemed to leave with a clear mind. Like when you came back from breakfast in a hotel and found that the maid had already made up your bed for you and tidied up the room.

On that particular day Joe Maguire knew all too well that it was going to take a lot more than a toasted bagel to solve his current problem. He remembered what his mother used to say to him when he had some problem when he was a boy – 'Just wait – the Good Lord will send you a sign and you'll know what to do.' Instinct told him that he'd come to the end of the road so far as the CIA and MK Ultra were concerned. But he knew how much they'd come to rely on him and that there was no obvious person to replace him. He wore too many hats, the army, the

Pentagon, the law, the CIA and the Senator. And above all his independence. Beholden to nobody. And the MK Ultra people were crossing frontiers of behaviour and action that he found had caused him more and more concern. The medics and the psychiatrists had taken over. They no longer served the needs of operators but experimented both in drugs and hypnosis just for the hell of it. By his standards they were not defending the USA but indulging their wildest mind-control fantasies. But he could see no way of controlling them. They didn't even stick together. Each one was hidden inside his own convoluted world.

Joe Maguire had had this feeling before. Coming back a stranger to his own people after Vietnam, when he had left the army and again when he'd left the law practice. Never a careful appraisal of what was wrong or what he disliked. Just the instinct to move on. He signalled to the waitress to bring him another coffee.

The patrol car slowed and stopped to watch the man weaving his way through the traffic on 42nd Street. The back-up officer got out and, holding up his hand to stop the car, he approached the man who was shouting in some foreign language. The man didn't resist as the officer took his arm and led him to the patrol car and eased him into the back seat before waving on the traffic and easing his body into the back seat alongside the man, who sat silent but breathing heavily.

'What's your problem mister?'

The man shook his head.

'Have you been drinking?'

'No. No drinking.'

'Where do you live?'

'Washington.'

'Washington? So what are you doing here?'

'I don't remember.'

The patrolman looked at the driver and said, 'Let's take him to the precinct and book him in on vagrancy.' He shrugged. 'He's got a heavy accent and he's probably an illegal. No green card. No nothing.'

NYPD Sergeant Bellamy stood with the patrol officer looking at the downcast figure sitting in the cell.

'We'd better search him for ID. Read him his rights and then bring him to interrogation cell 12.'

'Is that OK legally, sarge?'

Bellamy shrugged. 'When you've got a prisoner who can't even tell you his name you've got to do the best you can.' He paused. 'Maybe we'll have to get a medic to look him over. There's something wrong with him that's for sure.'

An hour later the Lieutenant had joined them.

'What have we got in the way of ID?'

'There's a typed confirmation from the Bureau of Translators that the holder is a competent translator/interpreter in Russian language. It's on official Press Association paper.

'There's an oldish notebook with a diary over a year

old. It gives an address in Washington and five or six local telephone numbers. The only one we've checked is the number of one of the Soviet outfits in Washington. There's a nude photo of a very pretty girl and on the back it says 'To dearest K from Simone.' There's a telephone number on the back.

'There's just over a couple of hundred dollars in cash and several cards. One for a club and the others are service providers. Plumbers and the like.'

'No actual ID? No name or address?'

'No.'

'Pass him on to Washington liaison. He's theirs, not ours.'

Detective del Rossi was not best pleased with the bits and pieces from the unknown prisoner.

He tried the number on the back of the girl's photograph and after three or four rings a sexy voice announced that Simone was not available until midday. He was invited to ring again later.

The telephone section got him the address of the subscriber and the name. The name was Tracy Palmer. It was charged at business rates. The address was a small alleyway off North Capitol Street near the Greyhound Bus Terminal.

He parked his car behind the terminal and headed for the alleyway. A panel at the side of the street door indicated that Simone's place was on the top floor. The stairs and the small landings were clean and well-kept and there was a geranium in a plastic pot outside Simone's door. He pressed the bell and waited. He was about to press the bell again when the door opened. It was the girl in the nude photo, and she really was very pretty.

'Simone?' he said.

'I don't recognise you, mister. I only service with recommendations.'

She moved back slightly as his hand went inside his jacket for his police ID. As he spread it open for her to inspect, he said, 'Detective del Rossi, miss. Could I come in for a moment?'

'Is this some kind of frame-up by those bastards in vice?'

'No, miss. It's just a routine enquiry.'

She stood back and opened the door wider.

'You'd better come in.'

She was wearing a towelling bath-robe. It was obviously well-worn but she nevertheless looked more elegant than most women look in a Versace dress.

She pointed to a cane armchair with deep cushions and when he was seated she sat opposite him.

'What's this routine enquiry all about?'

del Rossi reached inside his jacket and brought out an envelope which he opened and removed a photograph.

'Do you recognise this man?'

She looked for only a few seconds. 'Yes. Where is he? What's he been up to?'

'I was hoping you could tell me. What was he doing when you knew him?'

'Tell me what else you know about him. Why does he interest you?'

'I know almost nothing. I found your photograph with your name and telephone number on it. A paper

confirming that he was an efficient translator of Russian.'
He shrugged. 'That's about it.'

'You said you're a police detective, yes?'

'That's right.'

'Is that part of the CIA?'

'No way. CIA concerns itself with espionage and the police are solely concerned with local crime. If the crime covers several States then the FBI take over.'

'What else do you want to know?'

'What did he do for a living and when did you last see him?'

'He was employed at the Russian Commerce place. Said he was a freelance but when Grainger came on the scene that was when he kind of fell apart.'

'How do you mean?'

'It was like he was on some pretty odd drug. He couldn't remember things. His address. His name even. What he was supposed to be doing.'

'You said his address. What was his address?'

She shrugged. 'He lived here with me.'

'How did you meet him?'

She shrugged. 'I guess you realise I'm a call-girl. He came as a client. Was here almost every day. I quite liked him, he was kind and good company and in the end I let him move in with me.'

'But you went on with your business?'

'Of course.'

'What broke up the relationship?'

'It didn't break up. He was in one of those strange moods and one day he just never came back. I've never heard from him since.'

'How long ago was that?'

'A year at least.' She paused. 'He told me he was working on the side for the Americans and not long after he disappeared a guy came to see me. Wanted to know what had happened to our friend. Said he was from one of those outfits you mentioned.'

'The FBI?'

'No. The other one.'

'The CIA?'

'That's the one. He showed me an ID card. Then he started having sex with me. He still does.'

'What was his name?'

'Lew. Lew Grainger or sometimes he calls himself Lew Grover.'

'And you still see him fairly often?'

'Yeah. He was eager to make money and he talked me into doing porn films. Equal partners. Half a dozen different girls and other guys.'.

'You mean the guy from the CIA was in business with you making porn films?'

'Yes. I did the filming, he looked after the distribution. He's made it a good earner.' She shrugged. 'And he said it would have his protection.'

'What money are we talking about?'

'Twenty grand a week each. Sometimes more.'

'And the other guy has never contacted you?'

'No. Never. Sometimes I get calls where there's heavy breathing but the caller just hangs up. But you get used to that in my business.'

'You could get ten years or more if they got you.'

'He'll see that doesn't happen.'

'Where do you keep the films?'

'They're not films, they're videos. They're up in my attic.'

'Could I see them? Just the boxes?'

'There's a pull-down ladder in the next room. Just pull it down and go on up.'

When he came back to her he was still brushing the dust from his jacket.

She smiled. 'D'you want to watch one of them with me?'

'Thanks. Maybe some other time.'

She smiled. 'All sorts of guys buy them, including cops.'

He smiled back. 'I'm sure they do. But right now you and I need to talk.'

'What about?'

'I want you to take some time off. We'll pay for you to have a week's holiday. Any place you fancy. A police-woman will be with you all the time for your protection.'

'Protection against what?'

'I can't say at the moment but it's not concerning your businesses.'

'I've got clients booked in already.'

He smiled. 'Leave them a nice sexy message on your answer-phone.' He paused. 'How long do you need to pack? You won't need any money.'

'What if I refuse?'

'I didn't hear that. My report will emphasise that you have been totally cooperative and have had a guarantee of no legal action against your set-up.'

'My God. I expect Humphrey Bogart to walk in any minute.'

'Let's make it Paul Newman or Robert Redford.'

She laughed and stood up.

'This is crazy. I don't believe it. I haven't even had breakfast.'

'Have you remembered the guy's name? The missing one?'

She frowned. 'I think it was Kretski. Something Russian or Polish like that. Rudi. Rudi Kretski.'

The FBI was not much loved by local police in any city and apparently beneath contempt so far as the CIA was concerned. So it was with a special pleasure that Senior FBI Agent Crawley phoned the Senate office of Senator Heller.

'Senator Heller's office.'

'Senior FBI Agent Crawley. I'd like to speak to the Senator.'

'Can you tell me what it's about?'

'Just put me through to the Senator.'

'Is it business or personal?'

'Both.'

For a moment there was silence and then the woman said, 'I'll see if he's free to talk.'

Several moments passed and then a man's voice said, 'My secretary didn't get your name. Could you repeat it please?'

'Yes. I'm Senior FBI Agent Crawley at the Washington bureau.'

'Right. Now how can I help you?'

'Senator, I've some confidential information that I'd like to discuss with you. When can we meet?'

'Where are you speaking from?'

'I'm in the Senate foyer.'

'Come on up then.'

Senior Agent Crawley found the Senator an amiable man unlike his reputation as a bully. The Senator's secretary had brought in coffee for them both and as the Senator sugared his coffee and stirred it in, he said, 'I'm told by those who have experience of these things that FBI agents never come bearing good news. Are they right?'

Senior Agent Crawley smiled. 'I'll leave that to you to decide, Senator.'

'OK. The floor's yours.'

'I had reason to check on a mid-town address and the occupant, a young woman.'

Senator Heller sighed theatrically. 'Don't tell me, Mr Crawley. She's being screwed by some Republican Senator or half a dozen Congressmen.' He shrugged. 'I've heard it all so many times. It doesn't interest me.'

'I'm afraid it's not that simple, Senator.'

'It never is simple but carry on.'

'The reason for contacting the woman was to check the alibi of a man who had been detained in New York.' He paused. 'The arresting officer thought he was both drunk and under the influence of drugs.'

The Senator shrugged. 'A fair enough assumption these days.'

'Well in fact he's a very sick man and what he has revealed indicates a very serious security problem. The head of my section felt that I should seek your advice before I go any further.'

'You mean me as a lawyer or me as a Senator?'

'As a Senator.'

'So what's the problem?'

'The detained man's name is Kretski. Rudi Kretski. He was employed as an adviser to the Soviet Commerce Agency. So far as we can ascertain he is a Soviet citizen. He offered to defect to the CIA who took him up on it. The CIA officer who was in charge of him is a man named Grainger. Lew Grainger. Grainger was part of a CIA operation called MK Ultra and it seems that Kretski was used experimentally by Grainger to test human reactions to various drugs. During the course of this treatment Kretski disappeared until a few days ago when he was picked up by NYPD in New York.'

'Did the CIA try and find him when he went missing?'

'It seems Grainger didn't report that the man was missing. He wasn't involved in active CIA operations so nobody bothered about what he was doing for Grainger.'

'And your boss suggested you come to me because I have a reputation for criticising the games that the CIA get up to.'

'There is a little more, sir, which my people feel establishes the lack of control inside the CIA.' He paused. 'Kretski, when he was at his Soviet job, lived with a young woman who was a call-girl. When Kretski disappeared the CIA man, Grainger, virtually took his place with the girl. Not living at her penthouse flat but on a casual sexual basis and was also a partner with the girl in the production and distribution of porn videos.'

'Is the company registered anywhere?'

'Yes. And the girl and Grainger are registered as equal partners with a lawyer holding a balance of two per cent.'

'How many people know about all this?'

'Myself and four people senior to me in the FBI. The girl of course and one full-time FBI attorney.'

Heller leaned back in his chair, his eyes closed. Wretched and sordid as this was, it made his point totally effective about CIA needing to be brought under some political control. It would do incredible damage to the whole fabric of the CIA. And it would be a shameful finish for Joe Maguire. Still with his eyes closed he said, 'What did the FBI attorney say?'

'He said there was more than enough to start impeachment proceedings against Senator Maguire, and the Director and Deputy Director of the CIA.'

'Did he pass any other comment?'

'Yeah. He said the public wouldn't go along with the impeachment and would see it as more treasonable than what the CIA were up to.'

'Is your report in writing anywhere?'

'Yes. It's part of the case-file.'

Heller sighed, opened his eyes and leaned forward, elbows on his desk, as he looked at Senior Agent Crawley.

'Looks like it's time to sort the men from the boys, officer. Leave me a copy of your report.'

When the FBI man had left, Heller twice reached for the phone and twice he drew back his hand. He had looked forward for a long time to the day when he could settle his account with Maguire and the rest of them. But now that he knew he could do it just by a couple of phone calls it made him think clearly about the repercussions of what he could do. What was his real objective, to publicly disgrace a national institution or to bring down one man because of the man's open hatred of politicians and his indifference to those who didn't agree with him. At least Maguire was an honest man and totally unbribable. Nevertheless, he was a man who took the law into his own hands. He wasn't just playing for the wrong team. For a few moments Heller's thoughts about Maguire had an element of generosity but it was soon diluted, first to a kind of neutrality and then a flash of anger at the vague memory of some past, public indifference by Maguire to one of Heller's protests and complaints. Maybe there were other things that Joe Maguire should have learned way back in Saigon. Like the fact that all the world don't love a soldier.

The vague shadows of reason in Heller's mind soon gave way to the unfamiliar fact that it was his turn at long last to make the victory speech. It was a time for practicalities and planning, for assembling the troops and casting those players with speaking parts.

Chapter Thirty-Eight

A week went by before Arthur Heller realised that despite his damning evidence of abuse of the law and the constitution by the CIA, there were few who were ready to put their names to any form of legal action. Even the handful who were willing to be named were convinced that the pubic would be more interested in the porn aspect than the misdeeds of the CIA. The FBI were pressing him to take some action one way or the other.

Two days later Heller was shocked to read an unattributed report in the *Washington Post* that there was to be an investigation of the legal aspects of certain intelligence operations. The source was given as 'a senior constitutional lawyer'. The piece had all the indications of an inside leak and the finger-prints of the FBI.

When Heller had a call from the Department of Justice it was from a senior official who asked if it would be convenient for the Senator to attend at the Justice building at 6 p.m. for a meeting with Associate Justice Anne Cooper. When asked what the meeting was about the official said rather curtly that he had not been informed of the subject matter but warned that any mention of such a meeting to the media would be looked at extremely unfavourably. He sweated through the rest of the day but when he was shown into the magnificently panelled and furnished office of the Associate Justice he was treated with every respect and given a high-back chair facing her across a huge mahogany desk.

'Senator Heller, I haven't had the pleasure of meeting you before but I hope not to take up too much of your valuable time.'

She smiled amiably but Heller had been around Washington DC a long time and heard and recognised the echoes.

'I'm at your disposal, ma'am.'

'I'm sure that you read the piece in the *Post* about an investigation of the intelligence services, yes?'

'Very briefly.'

'I used to be legal advisor to a number of investigative committees and I know how the media love making mischief if they get half a chance. I gather that a number of people in and out of Congress and the media are attributing the leak to your good self.' She paused. 'Is that the case?'

'Of course not, but I have concerned myself about this kind of problem for several years now. People know this so I get blamed for all the leaks, true or not.'

'Is this all true do you think?'

'Can you spare the time for me to tell you what has caused the problem?'

'Of course. Do carry on.'

With the benefit of so much advocacy in his legal practice, Senator Heller presented a quite coherent version of the various strands of what had happened. When he had finished Annie Cooper was silent for quite a long time and then she stirred as if she had finished her thinking.

'So I suppose, Senator, you are left with the choice of saying nothing that would be detrimental to our intelligence services but forgoing the chance of removing your fellow Senator, Maguire, from his job which you think he does not perform properly. Is this the position?'

'Yes. You described it very accurately, ma'am.'

'Which would you rather do – bring down Senator Maguire or bring down half the government, and every politician in the house?'

'I'd prefer to just have Maguire removed.'

'Do you know Maguire well?'

'No. He's not my kind of man. Too sure of himself, too dictatorial, thinks he's still in boot-camp, drilling the squaddies. He has this strange belief that the CIA are the prime bastion of our defence against the outside world.'

'What do you think we should have as our defence instead?'

'Talking. Diplomacy. Politician to politician.'

'I see.' She paused. 'If I were able to persuade Senator Maguire that it was time that he retired and he went public on it. Would that satisfy you?'

'Yes. Certainly. If you think he would do it.'

'And no hints or leaks from your side about any of our intelligence services, yes?'

'Of course.'

She stood up slowly. 'He'll resign next weekend and he

will not have been pressured by me, you or anyone else. Just decided himself that it's time for a change.' As she walked him to the door she said, 'Send your file on this Kretski business back to the FBI man. It's officially their property.'

'Of course. As soon as I get back to my office.' He smiled. 'Thank you for your tact and cooperation. It was getting out of hand.'

Associate Justice Annie Cooper sighed as she closed the heavy door and leaned back against it. Men.

Chapter Thirty-Nine

───────◆───────

He parked his car alongside the chandlery and looked up at the sky as he switched off the car lights. It was dark blue with nary a cloud, and he knew it wasn't going to rain that night. He left the hood down just for the hell of it and then walked towards the river and the boat. The lights were still on on the boat. He ought to have realised when she insisted that she came to see him on the boat that it was one of his mother's 'signs from the Good Lord'.

On board he made himself a coffee and eased into the long seat on one side of the saloon table. There was a folded letter and a cardboard box already on the table. The box contained her gift of the charts and sailing service facilities down the river and then down the coast all the way to Cape Lookout. The charts were the equivalent of the Hershey bar his mother gave him when he did what he was told.

Annie had spoken so softly and so carefully that he knew she had rehearsed it all before. She recognised that it was unfair but she also recognised that it was the biggest gesture that Joe Maguire could make for the sake of the people he had protected for so long. Not ill-health as an excuse, nor spending more time with his non-existent family. Just a simple statement. He felt it was time to move on. Pastures new and all that sort of hogwash. He had always known that it would happen some day but he'd never imagined it would be about a man named Kretski who he had never heard of. He wondered what people like Adam Kennedy and his wife would think and say. And Angela.

He got his answer the next day after his resignation had been announced by the media. All the Kennedy gang had come to the boat with bottles of champagne and then taken him to the Italian embassy for lunch. Those people in Washington who cared about such things merely wondered why Maguire's resignation was so abrupt. And others were surprised to find that Joe Maguire, freed of responsibility, seemed to be a very contented man.

After their wedding at the embassy, he and Angela had moved across to California so that she could expand her gallery with new premises in Carmel. The boat had been shipped overland to its new base in Carmel Bay.

When Adele Kennedy had asked her husband why her sister was so close to Maguire, he had smiled and said, 'W.B. Yeats said it.'

'Said what?'

'I quote — "*A pity beyond all telling is hid in the heart of love*". Unquote.'

Ex-Senator Maguire still gave help to the Veterans Agency when it was needed and it wasn't long before several film studios were using him as a consultant on the constant flow of war films.

Patrick King is now an MP but still keeps his law practice going. Four pretty daughters make it necessary.

Rudi Kretski went through another protective routine to give him a new name and a new identity. He has a US government pension that allows him to spend most of his time learning to play golf. It's convenient to attribute his vagueness and loss of memory to the onset of Alzheimer's. He lives just outside Atlanta and looks over the Russian news media for CNN.

Charlie Brodsky was, as always expected, promoted to Director of CIA but the job was too political for him to enjoy it.

Joe Maguire only went back to Washington once and that was to read the eulogy for General Swenson when he was buried in the cemetery at Arlington. He was shocked at how few people attended.

Joe's resignation was treated by all concerned as the final marker for the end of all MK Ultra operations. It wasn't the end of course. The archives have been preserved in the basement of a well-known university and there is a laboratory in Florida where appropriate scientists operate for six-month stints 'just to keep the information current'. There are twenty-five outstanding legal claims for damages against the CIA on behalf of victims of MK Ultra. They've been on the books for over two years and there is no record of any litigant lawyer receiving a reply from Langley.

The intervention of the police officer from the patrol

car at Camber Sands had been enough to prevent the girl from carrying out the final deadly instructions given her in her hypnotic state by Fulton. It was much later, in her time with Dr Rosen, that he had wiped out all trace of the Karla operation without understanding exactly what he was doing.

It was only when he had more or less decided to ask the girl if she would marry him that he realised that all her documentation was spurious and had only been provided by SIS as a temporary measure. The thought of contacting Hargreaves at SIS and revealing that he had taken a patient under hypnosis as his mistress didn't bear thinking about. They could even prosecute him and that would be the end of his practice and his comfortable existence.

Dr Leo Rosen was not, despite his calling, a particularly meticulous man regarding sex between doctors and patients. The word therapy was commonly abused when the relationship could be described as consensual. Put bluntly, Leo Rosen was a moral coward by any standards. And, as so often happens in such cases, he and the girl are living together to this day. Perfectly happily and with more affection than many married couples. But he has to remember to call her Joanna, not Rosie.

**If you think that MK Ultra couldn't happen
try the Web on –**
                    mkultra cia

TED ALLBEURY

THE RECKONING

Katya Felinska is a beautiful and talented photo-journalist, passionately committed to championing the rights of the oppressed. Max Inman is a brilliant and incisive political journalist. They have been lovers for almost twenty years.

But Max is also an undercover agent, one of M16's most important sources on the real thinking of Russian and German leaders in the tense months leading up to the disintegration of the the Iron Curtain and the fall of the Berlin Wall.

Then things go wrong. Horribly wrong. And Katya must use all her courage and ingenuity to save the man she loves.

HODDER AND STOUGHTON PAPERBACKS

TED ALLBEURY

SHADOW OF A DOUBT

Accused by a malicious biographer of political interference, gross errors of judgement, adultery and virtual treason, former Director-General of M16 Sir James Frazer prepares to do battle.

But, in taking out a libel action, Sir James must submit to the rigours of a high profile court case in which his incredible past and turbulent private life are brought under intense scrutiny. Old wounds must be re-opened and long-standing secrets dramatically uncovered with devastating consequences for the security of the British Intelligence network.

In his compelling new thriller, Ted Allbeury tells of a brave and honourable man under siege from the modern scourges of sleaze and corruption, who must rely on the unpredictable verdict of a jury and run the risk of financial ruin in the desperate fight to clear his name.

HODDER AND STOUGHTON PAPERBACKS

A selection of bestsellers from Hodder & Stoughton

The Reckoning	Ted Allbeury	0 340 75094 4	£5.99	☐
Shadow of a Doubt	Ted Allbeury	0 340 71818 8	£5.99	☐
Aid and Comfort	Ted Allbeury	0 340 69644 3	£5.99	☐
The Long Run	Ted Allbeury	0 340 68215 9	£5.99	☐
Beyond the Silence	Ted Allbeury	0 450 64907 0	£5.99	☐

All Hodder & Stoughton books are available at your local bookshop or newsagent, or can be ordered direct from the publisher. Just tick the titles you want and fill in the form below. Prices and availability subject to change without notice.

Hodder & Stoughton Books, Cash Sales Department, Bookpoint, 39 Milton Park, Abingdon, OXON, OX14 4TD, UK. E-mail address: orders@bookpoint.co.uk. If you have a credit card you may order by telephone – (01235) 400414.

Please enclose a cheque or postal order made payable to Bookpoint Ltd to the value of the cover price and allow the following for postage and packing:
UK & BFPO: £1.00 for the first book, 50p for the second book and 30p for each additional book ordered up to a maximum charge of £3.00.
OVERSEAS & EIRE: £2.00 for the first book, £1.00 for the second book and 50p for each additional book.

Name ....

Address ....

....

....

If you would prefer to pay by credit card, please complete:
Please debit my Visa / Access / Diner's Club / American Express (delete as applicable) card no:

Signature ....

Expiry Date ....

If you would NOT like to receive further information on our products please tick the box. ☐